Returning to Love

Returning to Love

Lisa Phillips

Black Lyon Publishing, LLC

RETURNING TO LOVE
Copyright © 2012 by Lisa Phillips

Our books may be ordered through your local bookstore or by
visiting the publisher:

www.BlackLyonPublishing.com

Black Lyon Publishing, LLC
PO Box 567
Baker City, OR 97814

This is a work of fiction. All of the characters, names, events,
organizations and conversations in this novel are either the products
of the author's vivid imagination or are used in a fictitious way for the
purposes of this story.

**Cover Models: Jason Aaron Baca and Alex Navarro. Cover photo
by Mark Jenkins.**

ISBN-10:   1-934912-45-X
ISBN-13:   978-1-934912-45-4
Library of Congress Control Number: 2012936588

Published and printed in
the United States of America.

Black Lyon Contemporary Romance

For my father, David Gilbert.
I miss you every minute of every day, old man.

I have handled this Courage like a Coward
Thinking myself strong
To have weathered these confessions
Yet …
Without having given this Love a voice
Foolishly shrouding our Hope
The less I have had to face
Regret …

Dancing with the Illusions of Chivalry
Believing our Destiny
Romanced the Stars among the Ruins
Still …
Living the Beauty of this Mirage
I have grown to love this lie
Lost in never having to admit it isn't
Real …

And so my Scream rises forth like a Whisper
Wrenching my very Soul
I Love You, I love You, I Love you
Please …
Deeply knowing the madness of Without You
Fearing That silence
Between your breaths has left me
Cowardly.

—Ashley Adams

Prologue

*J*ulian Montgomery believed in hedging his bets until a sure thing presented a chance to do otherwise.

The potbellied banker from Baton Rouge didn't have squat. And the tech geek nervously blotting his sweaty brow with a cocktail napkin might as well have a sign that read *I'm in over my head* dangling from his neck. He thought because he banked a nice stash playing online in his dorm room, he'd find a backroom game and see how his run held. Apparently Lady Luck was locked and loaded, preparing to blow him right back to using his folks' credit card.

It was the pro to Julian's left who kept him from wandering out onto Bourbon Street in pursuit of anything even remotely entertaining. Trucker's cap, sunglasses, a toothpick clenched between his teeth, he was the whole package. He made a nice living prowling the circuit, and then rallied his earnings into a house in the suburbs complete with wife and kids. It was the sweaty scent of his anticipation spurring the smile curling the corners of Julian's lips.

"Welcome to New Orleans, gentlemen." Julian sailed three aces down, tossing back whiskey as he raked the pot across the table. Neatly folding the thick stash of cash, he tucked it into the back pocket of his worn jeans as he stood. The potbelly muttered curses under his breath, the kid slumped back in his chair seemingly relieved, and the pro spit the toothpick from his lips.

Julian had been playing in smoky backrooms long enough to know after scoring a pot that hefty, it was best to make a hasty retreat.

Sauntering out into the noisy bar, he winced as the first

mournful notes of the blues band on the stage rattled the rafters. Rounding couples swaying on the crowded dance floor, he tucked a bill into the bartender's jar, and passed another off to the pretty little waitress who plied him with drinks all evening. The sultry smile she flashed made him wonder if calling it an early night was really the way to go. Deciding that was the whiskey whispering in his ear, he let his tawny gaze roam over her regretfully as he stepped out into the warm night.

Slicking a hand through his dark hair, he lifted his face to the billowing breeze as he strolled the French Quarter. The flood of shock and misery had washed away, but he could still smell the suffering and survival that rebuilt the city that would not yield. Music poured from doorways of bars as tourists scoured shops while locals catered to them with gracious smiles. He turned another corner to disappear into the upscale hotel. Staff in neatly pressed uniforms busily scurried around as he made his way to the front desk.

"Good evening, Mr. Montgomery," the desk clerk greeted cheerily.

"How's it going, Bruce?" Julian ignored the huffy old broad checking in.

"Very well, sir." The clerk slid an envelope across the counter. "No other messages this evening."

Julian tucked the envelope into the pocket of his threadbare chambray shirt. "Thanks."

"My pleasure, Mr. Montgomery," Bruce said with a nod.

Julian crossed the lobby, punching the button of the elevator as his gut twisted into a slippery, jerking knot. He rode six floors with a couple groping each other like horny teenagers before finally letting himself into the lavish suite he'd called home for three months. It was the longest he'd been in one place in nearly eight years.

Going to the bar, he poured another whiskey, and took it out onto the balcony overlooking the swarm still buzzing Bourbon Street. He watched them, tourists and locals going on about their merry way on another thrilling night in the Big Easy. Taking the last sip of the whiskey, he strummed his fingers over his pocket, and fished the envelope out. Setting the glass on the wrought iron table in a corner of the balcony, he slowly tore it open, and pulled out the single sheet of paper.

It's time. Come home.
Ryan

The page fluttered on the wind as he closed his eyes, spinning down until it landed in the muddy mouth of the gutter below. Julian drew a deep breath, lifted his gaze to the waxing moon, then let the breath hiss out between clenched teeth. The grief was hideous, gripping his heart and squeezing until his next breath was almost impossible to endure.

He wouldn't remember stumbling through the suite, out into the hallway, onto the elevator. Shoving past a group gathered in the lobby, he raced out into the street. Dodging others wandering into his path, he ducked into an alley and sprinted out into the darkness. He stopped in a wooded glen more than a mile later, his breath coming in angry pants. He welcomed it, the pitch black shrouding him as he felt the sharp, jagged edge of agony splice through him.

All he knew to do was run.

But, he would not be able to run fast enough or far enough, a lesson learned long ago. When the clouds rolled back once more, pearly moonlight lit the clearing where he lie sprawled on the ground, clawing at the muddy earth as his body was wracked by choked sobs.

Chapter One

The cool, clear nights of early autumn finally graced the rolling hills and sprawling valleys of East Tennessee. The last whispers of summer still lingered in the brilliant burst of afternoon sunlight, but as night fell over the foothills of the Smoky Mountains, a chill settled over the picturesque countryside. The National Park was twenty miles to the south, the banks of the Tennessee River about the same distance the other way. In between were counties crisscrossing in a patchwork of rural splendor.

Julian turned off the highway that would twist and turn all the way through the mountains, the battered pickup chugging down the winding two-lane he could drive with his eyes closed. There was occasionally a charming farmhouse or rustic log home, but mostly pastures, meadows and thickets of trees flanked the blacktop. Another ten miles, and he made the left turn that brought him right back where he started thirty years ago.

Crystal Lake was just far enough off the beaten path for the stunning views of wooded hills and the sparkling water of its namesake not to be marred by rows of blinking signs, and close enough to catch the overflow of tourists looking for a more serene escape. It was the sort of place that defined small southern towns. The historic downtown square was hemmed in by the courthouse, post office, a few small shops touting everything from fresh flowers to gourmet coffee, and a couple of other old buildings that had been renovated into office space.

The town was founded by folks looking to keep life as quiet as possible. Turned out the tourist trade feeding many of the big cities and small towns across the state was a necessary evil. So locals went on about their quiet lives, extending as much southern hospitality as they could muster to the tourists plumping the local economy.

Julian stopped the truck at the curb of the square, sliding a pair of sunglasses over his eyes as he got out. Cobblestone paths ran in circles, beds of flowers and ferns spilling over onto them. Park benches and huge stones kids could scale were shaded by weeping cherry trees and maples just about to explode into burnished glory. The air cooled as he stepped out of the sunshine, mockingbirds swooping and squawking over his head as he stopped at the center of the square.

It was his earliest memory, sitting on a bench in this square with his father at his side, telling him how it was their ancestor who founded the place their bloodline called home for generations. There was such pride in his voice and in his tawny eyes as they roamed over the only place Aiden Montgomery ever wanted to be. For Julian there was always wondering what lie beyond the county line.

"Shame on you for sneaking into town like this, Julian. Now we won't have time to arrange a parade, or proclaim a national day of celebration."

The corners of Julian's lips twitched. He turned, sliding the sunglass from his face. "I'm sorry, Sheriff. But it isn't like you didn't know I was coming."

The sheriff came closer. To anyone giving them a passing glance, it would be no surprise to find out a mere eight minutes separated them. Their father always said find Julian, and Ryan would be right behind him. They weren't identical twins, but shared the same long, lean frame with just enough muscle to keep them from being lanky and the same jet-black hair. Where Julian avoided a barber enough for his to wave down past his collar, his twin sported the closely-cropped military cut preferred by lawmen.

Ryan slipped the Aviators from the bridge of his nose. It was the eyes that made the difference. Clear, deep blue eyes that crinkled at the corners as his brother smiled. Their mother's eyes their father always said in the hushed, mournful tone haunting his voice whenever he spoke of the woman his sons couldn't remember.

Dropping the glasses into the pocket of the tan shirt bearing the patch of his authority, Ryan extended a hand. "Welcome home, brother."

Julian slid his palm over his twin's, pulling him into a tight hug. He was indeed home. Slapping a hand to Ryan's back, he pushed him away to study him closely. "You look like hell."

"Good to see you too," Ryan snorted. Bracing his hands on his lean hips, he heaved out a sigh. "I haven't been sleeping much lately."

Julian felt his knees turn to water as he fell back onto one of the benches. Furrowing both hands through his hair, he avoided his brother's gaze. "I'm sorry, Ryan. I should have been here. I knew when I saw him at Christmas he was getting worse every day."

"The old man is fine, considering the last round of chemo damn near killed him," Ryan said casually as he sat down by his twin.

Julian stared at him for a long moment, his heart pumping like a jackhammer against his chest. "He's not?

"Nope." Ryan shook his head. "I'm not sure he'll see another Christmas, but when I left the house this morning he was bitching at Gran about runny eggs."

The sweet relief flooding through him turned to a whip of fury sprinting through his blood. "You sorry ..." Julian gritted out. His brother was up on his feet before he could knock him from the bench.

"Looks like somebody has gotten slow and soft while earning a living playing games and swilling whiskey," Ryan chuckled. Then Julian tackled, sending Ryan sprawling across the sidewalk. He grunted when a hard jab to his belly emptied the air from his lungs.

They rolled, throwing punches and trading insults, all around the charming square. When Julian struggled up to his feet, Ryan lifted a foot to hurl him back into a clump of ferns. He dodged the right hook he'd been evading since they were toddlers as he thrust a knee into Ryan's gut.

"What do you two idiots think you are doing?"

Julian was hauled up onto his feet by the collar of his shirt. When Ryan scrambled after him, a polished wingtip landed center of his chest, knocking him back into a cluster of wildflowers. Julian smiled, spinning on a heel to face his captor. "Hey, little brother. How's it going?"

Logan thrust him down onto the bench, his dark eyes spanning the square. He wore a neatly pressed, ivory button down shirt with a navy tie that matched the pinstripe in his trousers. Taller and even broader in the shoulders than his older brothers, good fortune assured he did not share their quick tempers. But, the dark hair, the same angular jaw and ready smile assured he was a Montgomery through and through.

"For God's sake," Logan gritted out, reaching down to grab Ryan to pull him up onto his feet. "The whole town can see y'all acting like a couple of kids on the playground." He dusted leaves and mulch off his brother's back.

"Get off me," Ryan growled, jerking a shoulder.

Logan's eyes pinned Julian again. "You're back, what? Five minutes before y'all are brawling?"

"Something like that." Julian spit blood into a bed of lilies, running his tongue over his teeth to make sure none were missing.

Logan glanced around again, nodding at an old couple rounding the square. "I realize any sense of decorum is wasted on you two, but I would rather my boss not look out his office window to find my idiot brothers tumbling around in flowerbeds, trying to beat the hell out of each other."

"He looked like hell before I laid a hand on him," Julian insisted, cocking his head at his twin.

Logan turned to Ryan. "You're the sheriff now. What kind of example does this set?" Before his brother could reply, he spun back to Julian. "I have worked myself closer to an early grave to become the youngest assistant D.A. in the state. I'll be damned if I'm going to let dumb and dumber humiliate me in front of the whole town."

"Give me a break," Julian drawled, leaning back on the bench. "It isn't like folks don't know who your daddy is."

"You sorry ..." Logan ripped off his pricey watch, hurled it at Ryan, and jerked Julian from the bench.

Ryan winced as Logan landed a driving fist into his twin's gut. "His brother being sheriff might have a little something to do with it too," he muttered.

When Logan reeled backwards from the punch to his jaw, he pushed him back into Julian. He slid the watch onto his wrist, holding it out to inspect it. Julian toppled into him, so he shoved him back toward Logan. "This is nice." He examined the watch closer.

When his twin landed at his feet and bloody drool smeared all over his boot, he jerked his foot away. "Hey, man! That's gross." Logan staggered as Julian swept out a leg to make contact with his ankle.

Ryan's gaze darted to the parking spaces at the curb. "Uh, oh." He reached down to jerk his twin onto his feet as Logan rose up onto his with a groan.

She came at them with the expression they learned to dread before they were out of diapers. Her silver hair was clipped into a chic bob skimming her clenched jaw, her piercing green eyes spitting fire. She wore a pair of black silk pants, a vibrant red blouse cinched at her waist with a silver link belt, and black alligator skin pumps that clicked along the cobblestone with her determined steps. She was a petite thing, still slim and fit at nearly seventy-five years old.

And Miranda Montgomery was by far the toughest Montgomery of all.

"What have I told you boys?" she hissed as her hands slapped to her hips. "You want to settle something by wailing on each other, fine by me. But, you will not do it in public. I am tired of going to fundraisers and book club meetings to hear how my boys are entertaining all of Crystal Lake with your own little fight club." She drew a fast, furious breath. "Ryan, get that mulch off your butt, Logan you have ruined another shirt, and Julian give me a hug before I bang all your heads together."

Julian moved into her embrace, dropping his head to place a kiss on her forehead. Her warmth, her scent, the loving way she held him was tangled with every cherished memory he had. She rushed in when their mother lost her battle with breast cancer shortly after Logan's first birthday, and hadn't so much as missed a step since. Gran was many things to a lot of people, but she made no bones about what came first in her life. She loved her boys. Sometimes being loved by her could be terrifying.

She skimmed a hand over Julian's cheek. "He'll be thrilled to see you."

He forced a weak smile as he stepped back, sliding the sunglasses over his eyes. "I'm not sure how long I'll be able to stay."

"Yeah, because there might be a horserace in Kentucky, or an all night poker game in Atlanta," Ryan drawled.

Gran lifted a brow as her eyes flicked to him. "You want to start something with me now?"

"No, ma'am," Ryan replied quickly.

"I've got to get back to the house. Your daddy will want a snack. He's mean as a snake when he's hungry." Gran dusted a hand over Ryan's back, and mulch flurried out around him. "Julian, you will be home for supper. You too, counselor," she added with a kiss on Logan's cheek. She turned, clicking her way back toward the Lincoln parked at the curb. "No more brawling, boys." Waving a hand sporting a diamond the size of a walnut, she slipped into the car.

"Well," Julian sighed. "She's still the toughest cookie this side of the Mason Dixon Line."

"Try the world," Logan muttered, straightening his tie. He looked at Ryan. "You give him the details yet?"

"What details?" Julian's gaze shifted back and forth between them.

"I haven't had time." Ryan tucked his shirt back into his khaki pants.

"Oh, that's right," Logan said with a nod as his long stride ate up the cobblestone path. "Y'all had to get the obligatory beating out of the way first."

"What details?" Julian demanded. He was hot on Logan's heels as Ryan brought up the rear.

Logan looked back and forth as they all hurried across the street, up the steep steps of the courthouse. Julian thankfully breathed in the cool air swirling around the old place as the boards of the wooden floor creaked under his feet. He waded through many stopping to welcome him home as he followed his brothers into Ryan's office.

Kicking the door closed behind them, Ryan skirted his cluttered desk to jerk on the cord at the bottom of a map. The map spun up to reveal a series of gruesome photographs held to corkboard with multicolored pushpins.

"Sweet Jesus," Julian whispered as he moved closer to the stomach-churning display. Ripping the sunglasses from his eyes, he studied the glossy photos. They were all shots of women, their bodies slashed and bloody, and their lifeless eyes staring into the camera. The resemblance was striking, the same long, dark hair and dark eyes. He drew a shaky breath, turning to face his brothers.

"What the hell?"

Ryan sat down in the chair behind his desk. "Three murders in two months. According to the coroner, probably the same weapon every time. Most likely a hunting knife, but we'd need the weapon to be sure." His brother stabbed a forefinger and thumb into his eyes as he leaned back in his chair. "He was sloppy the first time. He left a partial bloody print, but not enough for us to get any sort of ID from databanks if he's in there. Since then he's become much more proficient. The victims apparently knew him. No sign of forced entry or struggle."

Logan perched on the edge of the desk as his dark eyes scanned the photos. "They were locals. All of them."

Julian's stomach rolled again as bile rushed up into his throat. He swallowed hard against it as he lifted a shaky hand to swipe his chin. Turning back to the photos, he drew another deep breath. "That sort of resemblance isn't accidental, is it?" His voice was rough, sounding as bitter as the words tasted in his mouth.

"Doesn't seem so." Ryan looked at his younger brother. "He definitely has a type."

"Profile says he's not likely to stop unless he's caught, but there is a chance if we get too close he'll move on to other territory," Logan reported.

"Unless these victims are just practice and the ultimate victim is here in Crystal Lake," Ryan added.

Julian's knees finally gave. He fell down into a chair, his fingers curling tightly around the arms. "Have you talked to her? Have you warned her?" He stared at the photos, praying that sort of similarity was nothing more than a cruel coincidence.

Ryan shook his head. "We thought you would rather be the one to do that."

"Julian," Logan said as his brother stood. "There's one more thing." He averted his eyes. "He leaves a calling card. White tulips were found at each crime scene."

Julian swayed on his feet as another wave of panic slammed into him. Without warning, he fisted his hands in the front of his twin's shirt, dragging him up until they were eye to eye. "You ever even suspect she might be in danger and keep it from me again, I will be eating your liver for breakfast," he snarled. Thrusting Ryan back down into the chair, he strode across the office. The door slammed closed behind him as he stepped out into the hallway.

"So much for wondering if he still cares," Logan muttered as he stared at the pictures of the horror that had come to haunt their small, quiet town.

•

She knew he was coming.

Just as she knew when they were in the first grade the bad cold he had was more than a cold. She had her mother mix up an old herbal remedy to pass off to Gran to keep the pneumonia from taking any tighter hold of his little body. Just as she knew when they were eighteen, he shouldn't be in the back of Zane Miller's daddy's pickup out on the highway after a night of drinking beer and making up tales with his buddies down at the lake. She broke up that little shindig hours earlier than they would have on their own by marching out of the woods with a camera, swearing if they didn't hightail it home she had some interesting shots to share with their fathers. The car crossing the center line on the highway later that night didn't have a pickup to slam into, so the driver walked away with nothing more than scrapes and bruises after running off the road into a ditch.

Rowan always knew.

Because she knew his restless heart as well as her own, she waited. Sometimes patiently, sometimes with nothing more than the hope she'd finally summon the willpower to close her eyes and not know or feel ever again. She watched him walk away so many times she hated the thrill of knowing he was about to walk right back into her life. But, history had a way of repeating itself. Especially where Julian Montgomery was concerned.

Stepping back from the bouquet of roses, orchids and lilies, she eyed her work closely. Yet one more reason every bride in the county had The White Tulip at the top of her list.

She had been turning out bridal bouquets, funeral wreaths, elegant centerpieces to grace the tables of local dignitaries, and roses to ease a man out of the doghouse since she was ten years old. Her mother swore she had her grandmother's eye, the ability to take even the saddest clump of wildflowers, and yield a masterpiece that took folks' breath away. Rowan's entire life had been filled with flowers, herbs, gardens and the pride of knowing she carried on a business her great-great-grandmother started when horses and wagons traversed the rutty, dirt roads of Crystal Lake.

For Rowan, The White Tulip was one of the most cherished aspects of the only place she ever intended to call home. She was content to spend her days creating something beautiful that spoke of love, respect, well wishes, and even grief for a community where she knew most on a first name basis. Every night she watched the moon rise over the mountains, marveled at the stars falling in a rumpled drape over the hills that had been the backdrop of her whole life, and wondered why anyone wouldn't want to be right where she was at that moment.

And she long ago had to accept the life she loved and the man she loved might forever be at odds.

Hearing the bell on the front door jangle, she stepped out of the large back room lined with coolers, supplies and long tables filled with arrangements. The front of the shop was crowded with floral gifts, potted herbs, and displays of everything from potpourri and scented oils to lotions and herbal teas. Untying the bibbed apron from around her waist, she smiled at the teenage boy hovering across the long counter.

"How did it go today, Alex?" The kid blushed every time she spoke to him. He had only been working for them for a few months, making deliveries part-time after school. She hoped after he got to know her better, he wouldn't shuffle on his feet and mumble under his breath each time they spoke.

"Fine, Ms. Covington." He shook his head so his long, chestnut-colored bangs floated out of his big blue eyes. "I didn't get lost today." He set a clipboard with delivery tickets on the counter.

"Good," Rowan replied with a broad smile. "You're new around here." She pulled the tickets from the board. "It won't be long before you know the twisting back roads like the back of your hand."

"I hope so, ma'am."

He was as polite and respectful as he was quiet, so though Rowan had yet to meet the grandmother who raised him, she already liked her. They rented one of the charming little shotgun houses on the edge of town. Alex never spoke of what brought them to Crystal Lake, but she had a feeling his part-time job was more than just his grandmother's way of instilling a good work ethic. Because he was dependable, trustworthy and always willing to work over if she asked, she had given him two raises in three months. The fact she figured out finances were tight at home may have had a little something to do with it as well.

"Is there anything else I can do today, Ms. Covington?" he asked, glancing out the display windows at the uniformed officer loitering on the corner.

"No, thank you, Alex." She tried to keep the annoyance out of her tone as she watched the officer scan the downtown square. "I'll be locking up in a few minutes. You get on home. I don't want your grandmother to have to wait supper for you."

"All right, ma'am," he said with a respectful nod. "See you tomorrow afternoon."

"Have a good evening." She followed him to the door, flipping the sign to *Closed*. He waved as he headed for the beat up Ford parked in the lot across the street. She waved back, though her eyes were still fixed on the officer. "I don't know what you think you're looking for, Deputy Davis," she muttered under her breath as she flipped the lock.

But, she did know why.

Chapter Two

*J*ulian turned onto the gravel drive, the pickup rocking to and fro as it climbed the steep hill. Blackberry bushes and morning glory draped the barbed wire posted along the sides of the narrow, rocky stretch. As the truck topped the incline, the old Victorian rose up before him. Red brick and intricately carved white trim stood against the brilliant backdrop of the cool green water of the lake, the vibrant leaves of the mountains and the clear blue sky. Tall oaks flanked the house, flowers and herbs lining the brick walk winding up to the deep, covered front porch complete with rusted metal glider and a swing big enough to sleep in.

He sat in the truck for a few minutes, recalling how much of his youth had been spent on that porch. If he walked around to the backyard, he'd be able to see the house he was raised in. They were twelve years old the first time he swam that lake to get to her. They were eighteen the first time she let him lose himself inside her in a sunny glen overlooking the water. And they were twenty-two when she told him if he was leaving, it would be without her.

That was one of countless times he wondered who was more stubborn, him or Rowan Covington.

Tossing his sunglasses onto the dash, he got out of the truck. The scent of the rosemary growing by every entrance into the old place lifted on the breeze along with the smell of the flowers in the cutting garden on the south side of the house. They grew many of the ingredients for the wares they sold in the shop downtown, scented oils, lotions and candles to complement the thriving floral business the Covington family had run for generations.

He remembered helping Millie spread rosehips on tea towels in front of southern windows to dry, and gathering herbs with Rowan and Daisy before hurrying off to basketball practice. What little he hadn't learned about love in the rambling farmhouse across the lake, he learned in a drafty old Victorian filled with blooming flowers and cherished family traditions.

Before he could step up onto the porch, the screen door flew open. Her black hair, flowing down past her waist, was streaked with silver, her dark eyes lighting with the smile that brought another flood of memories to his mind. His father always said it was the gypsy blood that gave her such beauty, but according to Camellia, or Millie as she was more commonly known, it was the little bit of Irish on her mother's side. She wore a long, white cotton dress billowing out around her plump body and a wide-brimmed straw hat to shade her olive complexion. She had been harvesting sage. Julian could smell the pungent herb as she opened her arms, and he stepped into them.

"Oh, my beautiful boy," she whispered against his shoulder. Shaking her head with a throaty laugh, she held him at arm's length. "Though you're no longer that, I guess." Her eyes roamed his face. "You look like your daddy spit you out."

"Thanks, I guess," Julian chuckled. "It's good to see you, Millie." She cocked her head to one side as he looked over her shoulder into the house.

"She's out back. The pumpkin patch needed weeding, and she's itching to get mums into the ground."

He gave her a rueful smile. "I was wondering if Daisy was here."

Millie snorted out a chuckle. "Sure you were. She's still trekking across the New Zealand countryside. It seems you're not the only one with wanderlust, honey." She slapped a hand to his shoulder, and spun him around. "Go on! Get it over with so we can all stop dreading it. I know Gran is expecting you for supper, but you leave without telling me bye, and I will tan your hide."

She disappeared back into the house as he rounded it. Baskets of flowers and produce lined the back porch, the last harvests before the chill of autumn robbed them of the yields. A black cat scampered from between the baskets, crouching and hissing as he stopped at the steps. A tiny silver bell dangled from its collar, its wide green eyes narrowing as Julian snarled.

"Morrigan, be nice, please." The cat gave him one last glance before skulking back across the porch to curl up under a wicker chair. "You too, Julian."

Rowan was on her knees in the fertile earth. Her dark curls were pulled back into a ponytail that wagged across her back as she tugged weeds from the patch of pumpkins attached to wandering vines. She wore a white T-shirt that clung to her full breasts, a denim button down that swallowed her, and a pair of tattered jeans he was pretty sure she bought when they were juniors in high school.

He stopped where lush lawn met turned earth, sliding his hands into the pockets of his jeans. "Where did you get that shirt?"

Her dark eyes lifted, meeting his in the warm rays of the late afternoon sun. "What?"

"That shirt." He nodded, watching the tail of the button down trail through the dirt. "It's not yours."

Rowan looked down, and then turned her attention back to the task at hand. "I think it's Logan's."

"Logan's?" He heard the sharp slant to his tone, but didn't really care.

"Yes, you remember Logan." She ripped another handful of chickweed from the ground. "Six four, dark hair … He's your younger brother. Or have you forgotten him too?"

The shame brought a flush of heat to his face that rivaled the sunlight beating down on it. "That's not fair, Rowan," he bit out. "And for your information, I haven't forgotten a thing."

She closed her eyes, drew a deep breath and pulled the gardening gloves from her hands. "You're right. I'm sorry." Rising up onto her feet, she scooped up the basket of weeds.

He followed her down the sloping lawn to the compost pile. When he tried to take the basket from her to toss it onto the pile, she jerked it away. "I'm just trying to help," he snapped.

"I don't need your help." She hurled the weeds onto the pile, and grabbed the pitchfork. When he reached for it, she jerked it away. "Do it, and I will run you through."

"That's right." He watched her turn the pile. "It has to be your way, or the highway. I had forgotten that."

"Well now that your memory has been refreshed, how about you hit that highway again." Driving the pitchfork into the ground with all her might, she grabbed the basket and stalked back up the slope. "I'm sure there's a game of five card stud, or a cocktail waitress somewhere waiting for you to show."

He reached for her as her foot stomped onto the step of the back porch. Before he could make contact, she whirled, eyes black as midnight clashing with those as glaringly golden as the sun. A chill ran down Julian's spine even as he was drawn to her like a moth to a bright, hot flame.

"You could be in danger, Rowan," he said lowly as the wind ruffled the stray curls escaping her ponytail. He knew they would feel like silk against his fingertips and smell like vanilla. "I'm not going anywhere until I know you're safe."

"I am safe, Julian," she insisted. "I nearly trip over a police officer every time I turn around. And by the way, please tell your twin if he doesn't stop tailing me everywhere I go, folks are going to start talking. This entire town has been trying to marry me off to a Montgomery since we were in grade school. I wouldn't have any of you if you were served up on a silver platter with an apple in your big mouths, but I hate giving the grist mill anything else to speculate on."

"Like anybody would believe you'd have a thing to do with Ryan," he scoffed.

"Exactly," she purred sweetly. "Everybody knows Logan is the pick of the litter." He started after her as she marched across the porch. "Goodbye, Julian. Check back in on us in another year or so, if your poker games and cocktail waitresses allow!"

The screen door slapped closed in his face.

◆

Millie waved as the pickup disappeared into a cloud of gravel dust hovering over the top of the steep hill. Fishing the cell phone from the pocket of her dress, she hit redial, and pulled the hat from her head. "Hey, it's me. He just left." The hat sailed across the porch, landing on the old glider as she ran a hand through her long locks.

"Well, of course he was mad. And judging by the stomps I heard going up the stairs, so is my daughter." She wiggled a finger, and a fat black and white, long-haired cat crawled out from under the gardening bench by the porch swing.

"No. It will be a couple more days before she's back." She rolled her eyes. "Of course I'm sure. I think I can arrange for my own daughters to be under my roof when I decide the time is right.

What about Flo? Have you talked to her?" She sat on the glider, and the cat jumped up into her lap. "Good. I was afraid getting Ava back home would be the real trick." She dropped her bare feet up onto the gardening bench. "No, I'm not scared. Those boys aren't going to let anything happen to our girls. And don't you be worrying either. I'll talk to you soon."

Dropping the cell back into her pocket, Millie scratched between the old cat's ears as it stared up at her adoringly. "Oh, Jasper," she sighed. "The things we do for love."

•

Julian stopped the truck in the drive, dropping his forehead to the steering wheel. His gut was still churning and his body ached like a sore tooth. He hadn't spent more than twenty minutes with her, and he already wanted to crawl back on his hands and knees.

"I do not want Rowan Covington. I do not want Rowan Covington," he chanted as he lifted his head.

He was somewhat comforted by the site of Ryan's Jeep and Logan's Mercedes parked in the drive. No matter what he faced, it was always easier with his brothers at his side. He got out of his pickup, vowing he would never admit it to either of them. He didn't get the door closed before the big, goofy ball of golden fur with velvety brown eyes and a lolling tongue scampered off the porch right for him.

"Sit," Julian commanded masterfully. The golden retriever skidded to a stop, snorting happily as its bottom dropped to the ground. A fluffy tail thudded against the concrete driveway as it politely offered a paw. "Good dog," he praised as he leaned over to shake. The dog snorted again, letting out a hushed bark as it lifted both front paws into the air, and flopped over backward. Laughter rumbled out of Julian's chest as the dog scrambled back up. "You might be clumsy, but you sure are good looking, Prince." The dog let out a gale of barks, gleefully plodding along behind him as Julian went up the walk.

Nothing had changed.

The rambling farmhouse perched on a rise above the water was still white clapboard dotted with black shutters surrounded by green fields and thick forest. The barn Logan renovated into a living space sat to the left of the main house, the boathouse Ryan laid claim to when they were still teenagers overlooking the long dock jutting out into the lake glittering with the moonrise. Gran's flowerbeds, crowded with hydrangea, sweet peas and the brightly colored mums Rowan most likely planted, flourished in the creeping shadows of dusk. The old tire swing his father strung from a maple in the front yard, when they were too young to get up on it without a boost, still swayed in the evening breeze.

Julian hadn't even placed a grungy sneaker on the step of the porch before the screen door flew open. He stepped out, moving slower and more deliberately, but still like a man who knew where he had been and exactly where he was going. His once dark hair had thinned and was riddled with silver, his tawny eyes were hooded, and his face was lined with the pain of the sickness that ate at his body. But Aiden Montgomery was still a force to be reckoned with.

The screen door slapped closed behind him as his eyes raked over the man before him. Prince scurried to his side, the dog's tail wagging swiftly as Aiden dropped a hand to ruffle shaggy ears. "You're late for supper" he said in a gruff voice.

Julian shrugged a shoulder. "I know who really runs this place, old man. As long as I can smooth things over with Gran, you're the least of my worries."

Aiden's face lit with a wide grin as he lifted a hand. Julian took it in his, and was pulled into a desperate hug. He slapped his son's back with a chuckle. "How did you do in New Orleans?"

"Almost as well as in Tunica," Julian reported as they went into the house. "But those backroom games are hell on a man's nerves."

Aiden held the screen door open for Prince. "I seem to recall," he chuckled.

Gran was setting a platter of fried chicken on the table as they entered the dining room. Logan popped the cork on a bottle of Pinot Noir as Ryan reached for the bowl of mashed potatoes. Gran swatted his twin's hand, taking her seat at their father's right. Julian pulled his father's chair from the table, his brow creasing with a slight frown as the old man slowly lowered into it. Logan filled their glasses, taking his seat as Julian sat on his father's left. They had been sitting at this same table in the same chairs since he and his brothers wore bibs. Aiden lifted his glass, the candles in the center of the table adding a soft glow that gleamed against the crystal as they raised their glasses.

"To all of us being together again," Aiden toasted. His eyes met his mother's as he sipped the wine.

Julian filled his plate with chicken, potatoes, green beans he suspected were from Millie's vegetable garden, and the fluffy biscuits he dreamed about. Gran had a cleaning service come in weekly to help keep the place neat as a pin, but the food on his father's table was all her doing. Ryan groaned with pleasure as he devoured a thigh.

"Did you see Rowan?" Logan finally asked, giving his oldest brother a toothy smile.

"Yeah," Julian grunted, shoveling another bite of potatoes into his mouth.

"Did the sky bleed and the lake turn to ash?" Ryan mumbled around the chicken as he reached for the basket of biscuits.

"That's enough." Gran slapped his hand again.

"I only had two," Ryan defended.

"I mean your smart mouth." She lifted the basket, dropping another biscuit onto his plate.

"I told Rowan we'd be there around nine." Julian glanced at his twin. "You got somebody keeping an eye on their place?"

Ryan nodded as he slathered a biscuit with butter. "I can't imagine anybody having the nerve to go up against Rowan and Millie, but I've got Zane keeping an eye peeled."

"Good." Julian bit into a chicken leg. God, he had missed home. He wiped the grease from his lips with a napkin embroidered with his grandfather's monogram, and took a sip of his wine. "I assume nobody has a clue."

Aiden set down his fork, his face clouding with concern. "None. But, if those girls are harmed, I will deal with him myself."

"Girls?" Logan's fork halted in midair.

"Yes." Aiden lowered his gaze back to his plate. "They are like my own. Their fathers were the brothers I didn't have. Find that monster, boys." His golden eyes glinted in the candlelight. "Consider it my last request."

•

Rowan cut a generous slab of the pound cake she baked that morning, topped it with blackberry sauce, and poured a tall glass of milk. Morrigan followed her out onto the back porch, across the yard, into the woods. She stopped, her eyes scanning the looming shadows.

"Deputy Miller, I know you're out here, so you may as well come get this cake."

He appeared between two tall pines, the moonlight streaking along his gilded hair and shining in his green eyes. "Rowan, not so loud," Zane hissed. Lumbering toward her, he took the cake and milk. "Nobody is supposed to know I'm here."

"As big as you are, you're hard to miss." Scooping up Morrigan, she linked an arm with his. "You may as well come on up to the house. Millie will have a fit if she finds out you've been here and didn't say hello. The Montgomery brothers are on their way, so what's one more good looking fellow hanging around our kitchen?"

Setting the cat on the wicker chair on the porch as they passed, she smiled as he opened the screen door, and they stepped into the kitchen. She felt every muscle in Zane's impressive body tense, the fork on the saucer in his hand jiggling noisily. She reached up and caught it before it could clatter to the floor, but intentionally kept her arm linked with his.

"Evening, Ryan, Logan. Welcome home, Julian," Zane greeted with a nod.

Ryan's face split with a wide smile. "Evening, Zane. So, pound cake." He nodded. "Nice choice for a last meal. You just tired of living, or what?" He winced as Logan popped him on the back of the head.

Julian slid off the stool he was perched on at the island. "Aren't you supposed to be keeping an eye out?" He cocked a brow. "As in outside?"

"Well, Rowan ..." Zane held up the milk and cake. "See, she asked ..." When Julian's eyes narrowed, he set the cake and milk down. "I'll just get back outside." He spun toward the door, but Rowan kept a hand on his arm.

"I'll be out a little later, honey," she purred. Zane's eyes rounded as she gave him a sexy smile. He disappeared out onto the porch as she turned to the other men crowding her kitchen. "Y'all want some cake?" She pulled the lid off the cake platter, and reached for a knife from the block on the island. Julian's fingers closed over hers before she could grasp it.

"You and Zane seem awful cozy," he gritted out. Her eyes shot up to meet his, her face flushing.

"Julian, back off," Logan sighed.

"I would heed your brother's advice," Rowan warned as his fingers tightened around hers.

Julian leaned so close she could see the flecks of green in those golden eyes. "You don't scare me, honey. You never have."

"She scares me when her face gets red like that and there are knives within reach," Ryan mumbled around a hunk of the cake Zane deserted.

"Well, now look here," Millie cooed as she swept into the room. "All my boys gathered in one place." She went around smacking kisses on their cheeks. Her smile widened as she glanced back and forth between Julian and Rowan still standing off. "Seems like old times, doesn't it?"

Julian dropped back onto the stool as Rowan went to the coffee maker. "I assume Rowan told you about the murders."

"I didn't have to tell her." Rowan dumped coffee into a filter. "It's on the front page of every paper and all over the news. Believe it or not, Julian, we don't all crawl into a hole, waiting for you to show back up again."

"It doesn't bother you every victim bears a striking resemblance to you?" he asked tightly.

"Do you know how many women in this area have dark eyes and hair?" Rowan sloshed water into the coffeemaker. "Not to mention every woman who has ever lived in this house."

"That's exactly my point," Julian insisted. "Ryan will be posting uniforms around the clock." He looked at Millie, waiting for any argument from her. She simply shrugged a shoulder as she cut his brothers thick slabs of cake.

"Oh, good," Rowan purred. "Will Deputy Miller be included in that roster?"

There was a silent pause with the exception of the sound of Julian's teeth gnashing. Ryan stepped up to his twin, nudging him with an elbow. "It's your turn," he murmured out of the corner of his mouth. Julian turned his head slowly to meet his brother's gaze. Logan jerked Ryan out of his reach.

Julian slid off the stool. "I don't guess there's any reason for me to be wasting my time where it's not wanted." He kissed Millie's cheek as he passed her, the sound of his boots going down the hallway echoing around the quiet kitchen.

•

He was climbing into his truck, and the next thing he knew he was laid across the hood with Logan's nose pressed to his. "Hold on just a minute, big brother. I've got a couple of things I'd like to say."

Julian saw stars as his head banged against the hood.

"First, you don't get to mosey back into town when you're good and ready, and start issuing orders and ultimatums."

His head bounced against the hood again.

"Second, she's been here helping your grandmother take care of your father. Rowan has been here for your brothers while we watch our father wither away, and you cross the country chasing anything in a skirt."

This time when Julian's head made contact, his eyes rolled back in it.

"You are a man who has a whole lot to make up for. So drop the attitude because you and I both know I am the only one who can take your sorry butt, and I am chomping at the bit to do it!"

Logan let him go as quickly as he pounced. Julian groaned as he straightened up, keeping a hand on the hood to steady himself until his head stopped spinning. The thought of going back at his brother whirled through his mind, but as every word Logan said was the truth, he figured he'd just be making an even bigger fool of himself.

Ryan pushed away from the trunk of the oak he'd been lounging against, and settled a University of Tennessee baseball cap on his head. "I need a beer. Who's with me?"

"I'm in," Logan replied, though he kept his eyes on their brother.

"Guess I could use one too." Julian opened the door of his truck again, glancing at Logan over his shoulder. "And I don't chase anything in a skirt. You're confusing me with my twin."

Ryan grinned. "What can I say? The ladies love me."

Logan shoved him toward his jeep. "Shut up and drive."

•

She made a whole pot of coffee, and now there was nobody to drink it.

Rowan dumped the pot into the sink. Placing the top back onto the cake platter, she brushed crumbs from the island as she carefully avoided her mother's eyes. "I know what you're going to say."

Millie sat on a stool, placed her elbows on the island, folded her hands, and dropped her chin onto them. "What am I going to say?"

"The same thing you always say," Rowan said coolly as she dusted the crumbs from her hands over the sink. "I have to learn to control myself around Julian. No matter how much his cocky butt deserves it, I cannot allow him to goad me into acting irresponsibly."

"That's not what I was going to say," Millie replied drolly. "That's not what I ever say. That's what you say. You have always been far more reasonable and levelheaded than your mother. I always say hurl knives at his cocky butt until he wets his britches. Then we laugh until you feel better, and I don't have to kill a man I've loved like my own since his first breath."

Rowan smiled, rounding the island to straddle the stool by her mother's. "I guess that is how it usually goes." She laid her head on Millie's shoulder. "When will it get easier, Mama?"

Millie smoothed a hand over her cheek. "Oh, honey, nothing about loving anybody ever gets easier. And when you're talking about a man as stubborn as Julian Montgomery?" She shook her head. "Not a chance."

"He'll leave again," Rowan whispered. She closed her eyes as the dread that had become as familiar as her next breath fanned through her.

"You think so?"

"I know so. It's all I've ever known."

Millie brushed a kiss on her cheek. "His brothers need him. Even as terrified as he is of watching Aiden fade before his eyes, Julian won't turn his back on them. Maybe it will give him enough time to recall why being here is so important to you."

"What's important to me hasn't ever been the issue," Rowan murmured. "It's what's important to him Julian can't ever settle on."

•

Joe's Bar & Grill was on the sign, but to locals it was simply known as the roadhouse. The parking lot was two acres of gravel. Most nights patrons had to drive around a couple of times to find an available spot. It was constructed of barn board that had faded to a silvery hue with a red metal roof and a long porch extending all the way across the front of the building. Neon signs promoting beer brands flashed in the windows, and country/rock could be heard blaring for a good half a mile. Flo and Zeke Miller had run the place since her daddy, Joe, got old enough to cough up the recipe for his prize-winning barbeque, and retire up north with wife number five.

Julian got out of his truck as Ryan's jeep stopped beside it. ZZ Top crooned about legs as the wail of electric guitars floated on the breeze. His brothers flanked him as he threw open the door. Peanut shells crunched under their feet, the smell of beer and barbeque assaulting them as they acknowledged the many greetings shouted at them from those milling around pool tables in the back, the jukebox in a corner, and the long bar stretching the entire length of the place. Rows of high cocktail tables and booths along another wall were packed, so they waded through the crowd to the bar.

Flo turned from the taps with an icy mug with just the right amount of foam in each hand. Her long blonde hair might have already started to gray at the temples, but nobody would ever know thanks to Wanda over at the Cost Cutters. Her beautiful face had a few lines here and there, a few more around those brilliant green eyes, but she still had the body of a woman half her age, and was proud of it. That fact was most often evidenced by the tight tank tops and short skirts her husband of more than thirty years bought by the dozens. She set the beers before a couple of regulars telling lies at the end of the bar, and caught sight of Julian as she wiped her hands with a bar towel.

"Good Lord in heaven, look who is sitting at my bar!" She rushed over, cupped his face in her hands, and dragged him across the bar to press a noisy kiss to his lips. "Julian Montgomery, you look like your daddy spit you out," she drawled.

"So I've been told," he chuckled, settling back onto his stool. "It's good to see you, Flo."

"Zeke!" she screeched. Nobody even flinched. Hearing Flo screech her husband's name was part of the charm of the roadhouse. "Get your butt out here, and look who's home."

The swinging doors to the kitchen burst open, and Zeke appeared behind the bar. He was a big one, Zeke was. Six feet four, with the shoulders that had taken him all the way through UT on a full football scholarship, and a couple of years in the pros until his knee gave out on a sunny Sunday. He wore a red bandana tied over his clean-shaven head and a Harley T-shirt to go with his shiny pride and joy parked out back. He had been Aiden's wingman since they were in grade school. They loved nothing better than to bore everybody within earshot with stories of their misguided youth.

"Woman, I have asked you not to holler like that." Zeke examined a fingertip. "Every time you do, I burn off another layer of flesh. I'm telling you, you're gonna miss these fingers when they're gone."

"Oh, hush." Flo swatted at him with the towel. "Look there." She pointed a bright red nail at Julian.

Zeke's blue eyes warmed as he rounded the bar to scoop Julian from the stool into a tight hug. "Where the hell have you been, boy?" he demanded as he dropped his godson back to the stool.

Julian grinned. "I'd tell you, but then I would have to kill you." The smile faded from his face as Zane came out of the kitchen toting a rack of glasses.

"I am not going back in there until you do something about her," Zane insisted as he set the rack on the bar, and snatched a towel from a stack under the bar. "Spoiled little brat. Waltzes back in here like she owns the place." He rubbed the towel over a beer mug. "I don't care what her badge says. She runs her mouth at me one more time, and I'm going to shoot her with her own gun!"

"Hey!" Zeke barked. "That's my baby girl you're talking about, boy."

"Yeah? Well, your baby girl cusses like a drunken sailor, old man." Zane lifted a brow. "Wonder where she gets that?" He eyed his father as he set the glass into a cooler.

Right on cue the doors to the kitchen swung open again. Ava Miller had every red-blooded male in the bar looking her way. She was the woman with the body half her mama's age, and it was a fine one. A silky fall of blonde hair skimmed her shoulders, and it was the big blue eyes she got from her daddy that swept the place as the doors swung closed behind her. She shot out of Crystal Lake like a bullet from a gun into UT, then the police academy, and on to Quantico where she'd been trained by the FBI to wiggle her way into some of the sickest minds in the country. Firing her older brother a scathing glance, she tugged the hem of her plain white T-shirt down over the taut belly bared by the jeans hugging her hips, and hopped up onto the bar. Swinging her long legs over it, she placed a snakeskin boot on either side of Julian's hips.

"Hey, good looking. Where you been all my life?" she drawled.

Julian grinned, grabbed her by the waist, and jerked her off the bar into his lap. "I keep asking your daddy for your hand, but he always says no." He met her puckered lips with his own.

"It ain't her hand I'm worried about," Zeke muttered, rounding the bar to help his son dry glasses.

Ava looked at Logan as her mother set a frosty mug in front of him. "Have you asked for my hand?"

Logan shook his head. "Nope. I'm more interested in what your daddy is worried about." He leaned over to nip at her earlobe with a growl as she threw back her head with a throaty laugh.

Zeke rolled his eyes over at his wife. "You gonna let those boys get away with slobbering on your daughter like that?"

"She's all but begging for it," Flo snorted out.

"Wonder where she gets that?" Zane dodged the swing of his mother's towel.

Ava slid off Julian's lap, turning to Ryan as he lifted his mug to his mouth. "Hello?" She snapped her fingers by his ear.

"Hey, Ava." He licked foam from his lips, keeping his gaze trained straight ahead.

She stuck her tongue out at him as she turned back to his twin. "Have you seen Rowan?"

"Yeah," Julian grunted.

"All right then," she sighed, glancing at Logan. He shook his head as he reached for his beer. "Well, I haven't, so I'm going to head over there now." Leaning over the bar, she kissed her parents' cheeks. "Bye, jerk-wad," she said to her brother.

"See you, spoiled rotten, foulmouthed brat," Zane called after her as she went to the door. "I mean it." He nodded at his parents as he lifted the empty glass rack from the bar. "Either she goes, or I go." He disappeared back behind the swinging doors to the kitchen.

Flo rolled her eyes. "He's been saying that since the day we brought her home from the hospital."

Zeke gave his wife's bottom an affectionate pat, cocking his head at a booth being vacated by a couple of truckers. "Boys." They followed, sliding onto the tan leather seat as he set the bucket of boiled peanuts aside. "Zane tells me you still don't have a single lead."

"So much for confidentiality in my department." Ryan set down his beer, and reached for a peanut.

"What good is my boy being one of your deputies if I get left out of the loop?" Zeke blew out a long breath as he looked around the bar. "Now that Ava's home, maybe y'all can catch this bloodthirsty son of a gun. She's pulled what strings she can to keep any sniffing around here by the state and federal—"

"The state and federal can bite me," Ryan scoffed.

Logan closed his eyes. "I did not just hear the sheriff say that."

"Yeah, you did." Ryan lifted his beer. "And I would suggest you back Ava up, and pull any strings you got floating around, Mr. Big Shot. Nobody is going to swoop in here and piss on my party."

Julian slid out of the booth as he drained his mug. Setting it on the table, he looked at Zeke. "I'm more concerned about Rowan. I'm going to swing back by her place, and be sure the uniforms are keeping heads up."

Zeke nodded. "Julian!" He turned back to the table, the fear in Zeke's eyes like a punch to his heart. "This is wearing on Aiden. Sure would be a comfort to him if you were to stick around a while. Time is too short as it is. It damn near killed me and your daddy when we had to bury Remy. I'm trying to muster enough courage to go through that again, but I need some time, boy. I'm not too proud to ask you to give it to me."

Julian forced a smile. "I guess there's no place else I need to be."

Chapter Three

It had been so long since Julian saw the moon hover over the mountains he stopped, and let the thrill of it ease the apprehension weighing on him. He never got used to the sight of that mountain moon, or wondering if the valley soaking up the silvery light was where he was meant to be.

He sat down on a log in the glen, bracing his elbows on his knees. He remembered the first time Gran told him how proud he should be, knowing one day he could follow in his father's footsteps. He was only five years old at the time, so he had no idea what that meant. As he got older, he learned exactly what it meant. It meant living under a microscope, even in a place as closely guarded as Crystal Lake. It meant carrying on the proud tradition of guns and badges that riddled his family for generations.

He went so far as the police academy after college, even smiled for Gran's constantly flashing camera the day his father swore him in as a deputy. But, after a few months of pulling over traffic offenders and running teenage boys away from the lake by threatening to arrest them for underage drinking, he began to wonder if the life he always assumed would be his was one he wanted.

It was Remy's funeral that brought him back to the mountains the first time he put as much distance between him and Crystal Lake as he could stand. Folks were reeling with the thought of how a tough lawman like Remy could be there one day, and gone from a sudden heart attack the next. All that grief, watching the people he loved mourn their own, drove Julian right back over the county line. The memory of his father rocking Rowan in his arms as they both wept with the horrific loss of her father had Julian's pickup doing ninety until he reached the west coast.

Being in Crystal Lake was hard enough, loving and mourning and brawling with his brothers ... And then there was the constant fear he wouldn't ever be able to live up to the expectation of who he was born to be. That was Aiden Montgomery. How the hell was anybody supposed to live up to that?

He turned his head as her scent rode the breeze rustling the dried leaves spread around his feet. Wondering if there would ever be a time when knowing she was near wouldn't make his heart pound and his mouth water, he watched her move out of the darkness into the fragile light. Even if he closed his eyes, he would still see her standing there, long, dark curls he wanted to wrap around his hands and haunting gypsy eyes ... Rowan Covington's hold on him began with a chaste, hurried kiss between twelve year olds, and was still the one tie to Crystal Lake he'd never been able to wrangle free from.

She sat by him on the log, lifting her face to the moon's tender glow. "I had a feeling you would be here. I come here to think sometimes too."

He linked his fingers together tightly to keep from grabbing her. "I always find it sort of ironic as this is the place I first learned what it was like not to be able to think at all."

"Julian," she sighed with a shake of her head.

"I'd appreciate it if you didn't say that was a long time ago," he murmured. "It was a long day, and it's looking like it's going to be an even longer night." He could feel her eyes on him, but if he looked at her he might start begging.

"It isn't just about us anymore."

"It never has been." He gathered a handful of leaves, crumpled them in a palm. "That was part of the problem. And you damn sure weren't going anywhere to find out if we could be us outside Crystal Lake."

"Shirking my responsibilities and walking out on those I love isn't worth anything to me." She was mad now. That he could deal with.

"How's that worked out for you, Rowan? Your sanctimonious pride keeping your bed warm at night, or is Zane taking care of that?" He caught her hand before it could make contact with his cheek, felt the fury shimmy from her heart to his. His eyes met hers in the shadows as the moon dipped down over a tall pine. "I win, darlin," he whispered. "You just gave me good reason."

Before she could respond, he tumbled her off the log, and into a bed of leaves and pine needles. His mouth crushed hers. He decided whatever the price, it would be worth it. He was sick and tired of being tortured by the memory of her warm, sweet mouth and the feel of her body going soft and hot under his. He groaned as memories and that moment tangled into a throbbing need pulsing through him. Her nails raked his back as her hips rolled under his. The pleasure was so achingly painful he shuddered with another long, low groan.

Moonlight shot through the branches of the pine as her eyes gleamed dangerously. Her knee made contact, another groan echoing around them as he rolled off her into a fetal position.

"I win, darlin," she panted. "And I am not going to be the consolation prize for you finally showing up to do right by your family. They need you, Julian, but I sure as hell don't."

She disappeared back into the darkness as thunder rumbled over the mountains.

•

Ava stood at the window, watching lightning race across the sky. "Uh, oh," she moaned.

Millie set the tray of homemade blackberry wine and warm sugar cookies on the coffee table. "Is Julian with her?"

"Nope," Ava mumbled as she chewed a lip. "Judging by the way she's marching up the walk, I hope he's somewhere ducking for cover." She winced as another boom of thunder shook the house.

"Well, I'm off to bed," Millie sighed.

"No, you're not." Ava turned from the window. "You get back down here right this minute," she hissed. Millie flew up the stairs, disappearing into her room as Rowan stomped into the house. Ava grabbed the plate of cookies.

"I hate him," Rowan swore as Ava lifted a cookie to her mouth.

"Yeah well, love and hate, fine line and all." Ava raked leaves from her hair with her fingers as Rowan devoured the cookie. "On the bright side, it's been a while since I had to pick the evidence of how much you hate Julian out of your hair."

Rowan took the plate of cookies, nodding at the tray. "Shut up and pour."

Ava quickly splashed wine into a glass. "If you're this mad, how bad off is he?" She offered the glass, filling another for herself.

Rowan sat down on the sofa, balancing the plate of cookies in her lap as she took a gulp of wine. "Let's just say it will be morning before he's walking upright."

Ava squeezed her eyes shut as she sipped the wine. "At the risk of incurring further wrath, may I say he's having a really rough time right now?"

Rowan's lips curled with a snarl. "I know that Ava. Knowing that is why I went to find him in the first place. Had we been able to discuss the situation like rational adults rather than rolling around on the ground like teenagers pawing each other in the dark, I wouldn't be sitting here stuffing my face with cookies and washing them down with wine."

"I've missed you," Ava replied with a sweet smile.

"I've missed you too." Rowan leaned over, kissed her cheek, and shoved another cookie into her mouth. "You know, I deserve to be more than a distraction for a man who is having a difficult time."

"Yes, you do." Ava lifted her glass with a nod.

"Like I told him years ago, there's nothing outside Crystal Lake I can't find right here."

"No, there is not." Ava took another sip of wine, reaching for a cookie. "Well, at least not for you."

"Because there is more to life than Julian Montgomery," Rowan insisted.

"Damn straight," Ava mumbled.

"Now that he's back, I'll just have to show him." Rowan nodded as she raised her glass.

"You sure will." Ava frowned. "How exactly are you going to do that?"

Rowan bit into another cookie. "I don't know yet, but I'll figure it out as I go."

Ava set her glass aside. "I think it's time I tell you something."

Rowan set the plate of cookies on the coffee table. "What?" When her friend hesitated, she lifted a brow. "Ava?"

"Julian isn't just a card shark drifting all over the country, honey. I suppose he let everybody think that, especially Gran and Aiden, so they wouldn't worry so much."

Rowan swallowed hard. "Then what exactly is he?"

"He's been a special agent with the FBI since he left Crystal

Lake. The only reason I know is we've been involved in a couple of the same cases. I swore to him I wouldn't tell anybody here."

"Why are you telling me now?" Rowan asked softly.

"I don't want you to take his concerns for your safety lightly." Ava took both her hands. "I don't want you to take any of our concerns lightly. Given he's a local, Julian is probably the most qualified to handle this case, which is the only reason Crystal Lake isn't flooded with federal agents right now. This maniac is a serial killer, Rowan. I was able to convince the feds Julian and I, as well as the local authorities, can handle this. But it's personal for all of us. That won't make it any easier."

"Why are you all so sure I'm a target?" she asked shrilly.

Ava drew a deep breath. "Ryan has been able to keep it out of the media so far, but serial killers often leave a signature of sorts at crime scenes, something to let law enforcement know it's their handiwork." Rowan's face paled. "In this case each victim has been found with a single white tulip in her hand."

Rowan's mouth went dry, so she lifted the wine to it with a shaky hand. She wasn't sure which was worse, all the years she accused Julian of being a shiftless gambler ignoring his family for the thrill of chasing women and poker games, or knowing she might be the target of a deranged murderer. Somehow wrongly judging him was worse. He never said a word, never defended himself, and never offered any explanation whatsoever. Maybe after all this time he didn't care enough about her opinion of him for it to matter.

"Rowan." Ava cupped her shoulders in her hands. "Honey, until we catch this maniac, you have to be very careful."

"Maybe it's just coincidence. Maybe the tulip means something else all together."

Ava scooped her golden hair away from her face with a heavy sigh. "I might buy that if it weren't for the victims looking so much like you. We are going to catch him. We'll work together." She smiled wanly. "As terrified as I am for you, it's good to be home."

Rowan pulled her into her arms. "I'm so glad you're here. Everything has always been easier with you by my side."

•

Aiden heard the front door close and heavy footsteps coming up the stairs. He closed his eyes as the door opened. Julian crept toward his bed to pull the blanket up over his shoulders. "Sleep well, old man," he whispered before tiptoeing back to the door. When it quietly closed behind him, Aiden reached for the cell phone.

"He's home," he murmured into the phone. "I don't know for how long this time. Have you talked to Millie?" He threw back the blanket as he sat up. "Good. Ava might be able to calm Rowan down before there's too much property damage." He chuckled, laying a hand to his chest as wracking coughs seized him. "I'm fine," he assured. "And let's take this one couple at a time. The only one more hardheaded than Julian is his twin. Yes, I've met Ava," he chuckled again. "She's almost as dangerous as her mother. We've been patient this long." He settled back against the pillows. "There's time. I've always said I wouldn't go out of this world until I knew my boys had the right one to hold on to when I did. Sleep well, my friend. I have a feeling we're going to need our strength."

•

Julian sat in the porch swing, tipping the beer bottle back. He saw Logan and Ryan dash from the jeep as the rain came down in sheets, and scramble into their places. The barn was dark, which meant his little brother had to be at the office early. A light still shone in the boathouse, which meant Ryan was pouring over the facts of the case. His brothers chose their vocations before they were out of middle school. Ryan watched enough old reruns of The Andy Griffith Show to think being a small town sheriff was cool, and Logan always argued Andy was better as Matlock. Julian wondered what they would have turned out to be had Gran not had such a crush on old Andy and their father wasn't police chief, then mayor.

Speak of one of the devils ...

He wasn't surprised to see Gran step out onto the porch wearing a thick bathrobe over her silk pajamas to ward off the damp chill. All his life, within ten minutes of his butt hitting this swing, she appeared to find out what he was stewing over. It was mostly because she loved him more than life, but there was also the need to keep Millie and Flo up to speed. God forbid he have a thought and those three not have a chance to gnaw on it a while.

She was halfway across the porch when a mournful whine sounded from the other side of the screen door. Gran huffed, rolled her eyes, and went back to open the screen door. Prince snorted happily, trotting around her. "Get out from under my feet, you silly old thing," she fussed. She pointed a finger, and the golden scampered over to plop down at Julian's feet. "When I fall and break a hip, it will be that dumb dog's fault." She sat by Julian, tugging her robe closer around her. "Mercy it's getting cold quick." She smiled. "Your granddaddy would say it's because the wooly worms are ..." She waved a hand. "Something, or another."

"Is that anything like the cold spells in spring you call blackberry winter, dogwood winter, and something, or another?"

"Julian Montgomery, we did not raise you to be disrespectful to your grandmother," she said, smacking a palm to his thigh.

"Yes, ma'am," he muttered around the lip of the beer bottle. He watched the rain slow to a gentle shower. "Are we going to talk about what's worrying me, or what's worrying you?"

"As I think we're both worried about the same things, let's talk about your daddy first," Gran drawled. "He knows, Julian. We all do, so you can stop the aimless gambler routine."

The beer bottle nearly slipped from his hand. "How do you know?" His voice quivered with fury. He loved Ava like a sister, so he hoped like hell he wasn't going to have to strangle her.

"Logan. One of his former law school buddies is a federal prosecutor. He assumed your brother knew. Told him how you wrapped up some case in Nashville, handed over a hit man with enough evidence to lock him away for life. The only reason your father and brothers told me is when you didn't show for Easter, I threatened to track you down, and give you a good spanking."

He reached for her hand, lacing his fingers with hers. "I didn't tell you for good reason, Gran. I deal with some pretty shady folks at best and monsters at the very least. The fewer people who know what I do the better for all of us." He looked up to find dark clouds shifting enough to reveal a patch of stars. "At least until now, I guess."

"Your brothers seem to think these murders might be a warning to you," she murmured as her fingers tightened around his.

He drained the beer bottle. "Other than my family, Rowan would be the ultimate target." The alcohol buzzing his brain did little to ease the fear slithering through him. "This means he's done his research. And he's pissed."

She kissed his cheek as she pushed up onto her feet. "You'll stop him. I'm sure of it." Prince followed her back to the door.

"How are you so sure?" he asked as the fear reared inside him once more.

She held open the screen door for the dog, giving her grandson a smile over her shoulder. "I know because Rowan has always been the one to hold your heart here in Crystal Lake. Follow your heart this time, Julian. It will not only keep Rowan safe, it will grant a dying man his last wish."

•

Rowan nearly sloshed her tea down the front of her brown turtleneck as Ava dragged her into Ryan's office. He was at the coffeepot pouring for his brothers as Logan perched on an edge of his desk, and Julian sat in a chair with his battered boots propped up on another edge. Ava shrugged out of her khaki barn coat, tossing it over the back of another chair. "Sheriff," she greeted coolly. She was all FBI business this morning in a starched white blouse and slim black slacks. Well, except for the red eel skin boots.

"Special Agent Miller," Ryan replied with a nod. He handed his brothers steaming mugs, and filled another for himself. "Morning, sugar." He kissed Rowan's cheek, pulling a chair up beside the one behind his desk for her. It was more an attempt to rankle Julian than chivalry. "Let's be sure we're all on the same page." Ryan set his coffee down, and gave Ava a tight smile. "This office runs this investigation. Nothing said here leaves these four walls."

Ava rolled her eyes over to Logan. "You want to tell Sheriff Pissing Contest, or you want me to do the honors?"

Logan threw up both hands. "All right, let's go ahead and get this out of the way. When it comes to this case, leave your egos at the door." He glanced at Julian. "All of you. I've been watching the four of you grapple my entire life, and as entertaining as it has been, I've got the DA breathing down my neck. Ryan, like it or not, Ava is keeping the feds off your tail. This case screams serial killer, and if it weren't for her, you'd be jockeying coffee and answering phones while the federal agents took over." When there wasn't a single voice of dissent, Logan nodded. "Good. Ryan, why don't you start?"

His brother flipped open a file, then glanced at the photos Rowan was trying not to look at. "All the victims were locals, strikingly similar in appearance and approximately the same age. The perp either knew them, or laid in wait to surprise them, as there were no signs of struggle. Each victim was killed by…" He hesitated as Rowan closed her eyes tightly. "Cause of death in each case was a single stab to the heart, though exactly sixteen stabs were delivered to each victim." His eyes flicked to his twin. "Does Rowan really need to be here for this?" She was white as a sheet, her fingers trembling around the foam cup in her hand.

"Yes," Julian replied sternly. "She keeps insisting we are all overreacting. Maybe once she knows the facts, she'll take this a little more seriously."

"I'm fine, Ryan." Rowan laid a hand over his. Her eyes met Julian's. "Just because I don't scare easily doesn't mean I'm stupid, Special Agent Montgomery."

Julian turned to Ava, raising a dark brow. "She was going to find out eventually," Ava insisted. "I know Logan told your family, so now maybe we can all stop tiptoeing around, and catch this maniac." Going to the photos still pinned to the board, she looked them over slowly. "There are a few things that don't settle right with me."

Julian went to her side, his eyes scanning the detailed shots of the crime scenes. "Such as?"

"Typically serial killers draw out their attacks, torture their victims. A victim's pain and suffering is usually their motivation. These women were killed quickly, and then further mutilated after death."

"Maybe he figured he didn't have time," Logan proposed.

Ryan shook his head. "He's too calculated for that. All the victims lived alone. He wouldn't have been sloppy enough to strike when he would need to hurry."

"Then there's the exact number of stab wounds in each victim." Ava met Julian's gaze. "Sixteen exactly, each time."

"Another message of some kind," Julian murmured. He turned to Rowan. "Does that number hold some significance I'm not recalling?"

"Not that I know of," she replied with a shake of her head. The thought of three women's lives ended so viciously to send a message had her stomach rolling sickly.

"What if the perp killed them quickly out of fear of being overpowered?" Ava asked suddenly.

"Come on," Logan responded skeptically. "The victims were all less than five six and weighed in at no more than a hundred twenty pounds. Even if he's not the burly type, he wouldn't have much trouble overpowering women that size."

"Unless he is a she." Julian's eyes locked with Ava's once more.

She nodded, turning back to the photos. "It would explain the brutality of the attacks. Stabbing is personal, often indicative of revenge and rage."

Logan frowned. "Isn't a woman perpetrating this sort of slaughter rare?"

"Very," Ava answered. "But, there's much to be said for a woman scorned."

"Jesus," Ryan muttered. "We haven't even considered that." He rolled his eyes over at his twin. "Although a woman scorned would make more sense if this is all directed at you."

"Isn't that the pot calling the kettle black?" Logan glanced back and forth between his brothers.

"I don't think it's that sort of scorn." Ava perched on the edge of the desk to flip through Ryan's file. "I think this is an eye for an eye."

"Okay, can we please stop with the clichés?" Logan stood to pace back and forth.

"If the tulips left at the scene are a clear indication Rowan is the ultimate target, there is a reason these other women were murdered first," Ava mused. "Besides the serial killer head game aspect, which doesn't fit with the attacks. I just don't buy this being the typical serial killer. Too many of the common motivations are missing."

"Julian had to be lured back," Rowan finally said. "Possibly you as well, Ava." She looked at the friend she knew loved her like a sister. "You said you and Julian worked a few cases together over the years. What if this is about killing two birds with one stone?" She forced a smile for Logan. "Sorry about another cliché."

"As it may be a brilliant one, I'll let it go, sweetheart," Logan said, examining the photos. "It makes sense. The perp knew both of you would come running the minute you suspected Rowan was in danger. Even if these slaughters are only directed at one of you, it's more than we've had to go on so far." He fished his cell out of the breast pocket of the jacket of his pricey suit. "I'll make a couple of calls, and have all the cases you've both worked since signing on with the FBI sent to us."

"Sifting through all those will take a while," Ryan sighed.

"We'll start with the ones we had in common," Julian proposed. Reaching for Rowan's hand, he hauled her from the chair. "I think we've all had enough for one morning." She didn't argue as he ushered her to the door. "Call me when those files arrive," he instructed over a shoulder.

•

Rowan was pleasantly surprised when she wasn't given a strict list of what she was and was not allowed to do. Issuing orders was Julian's strong suit. He said nothing as he escorted her to her car, and then climbed into his pickup. Still baffled by the lack of bullying, and sick at her stomach over all she saw and heard in Ryan's office, she popped her head into The White Tulip to be sure her mother didn't need another set of hands. Assured she deserved a rare day off, she didn't fuss as Millie shooed her back out the door. When Julian's truck turned off onto their drive a few minutes after her dinged Honda, she knew why she hadn't gotten a sermon.

She got out of the car, reaching back in for her purse. When she turned, he was right beside her. "No wonder I was spared." He trailed her up onto the porch. "You were following me."

"Old habits die hard," he muttered as his eyes scanned the yard. He peeked in a window through the lacy curtains.

"Logan had a good point about all the clichés," she drawled as she unlocked the front door. He stepped in front of her, pulling a revolver from the waistband of his worn jeans. "Is that really necessary?"

He placed the tip of the gun barrel to his lips as he dragged her into the foyer. She was shoved up against a wall, and knew to stay there as he did a sweep of the first floor. By the time he cleared the second floor and attic, she was in the kitchen chasing aspirin with a cup of cold coffee. He sauntered into the sunny room, tucking his gun back into his waistband. Tossing a duffle bag onto the old harvest table, he went to the coffeemaker.

"Oh, no." She shook her head as she eyed the bag. "Absolutely not!" Marching to the pantry, she fished a handgun from a saltine box. "I have another under my bed, as does my mother. And you know good and well we can shoot a fly off a bear's butt at thirty paces. My daddy saw to that by the time I was twelve, just as yours did. Go home, Julian."

He filled the coffee maker, and hit the button. Turning to face her, he leaned back against the counter with the slow grin that turned her bones to jelly. "Millie said she'd feel better if I stayed here. Gran and Flo think it's a good idea too."

"Well of course they do," she snapped. "Didn't Zeke and Aiden get a vote too?"

"Yeah, but nobody is scared of them," he drawled as he crossed his arms over his broad chest.

She placed the gun back in the cracker box, and returned it to the shelf. "I mean it, Julian. I don't want you here."

It was surprising how quickly he could move, how fast the long, tough length of him could be pressed up against her as those golden eyes flashed with everything from fury to passion. He shook her, her head tilting back until there was only a breath between them.

"At the moment, I am not concerned with what you want, Rowan. You were the one who said it isn't just about us anymore. Three innocent women died, possibly as a result of me, or Ava, or both of us. Do you really think I am going to risk watching her go through losing you? It would break her." His fingers tightened around her shoulders, then slid along her arms. "It would break all of us," he said roughly as he backed away. "I promised Millie I would repair that rotted step on the porch." He disappeared out the backdoor before she could reply.

She took a moment to get herself under control, to let the bounding beat of her heart slow to a normal pace, before going to the phone. She watched him through the window over the sink as he carried her father's old toolbox out of the shed, up onto the back porch. "I know what you're doing, old woman," she hissed into the phone when her mother answered. "You and your partners in crime went behind my back!"

Rowan pulled the roast turkey out of the fridge. "There are uniformed officers scattered all over our property, mother." She tossed cheese, lettuce and a tomato onto the island. "The White House isn't as closely guarded as we are these days." Setting a jar of mayo and pickles out, she slammed the refrigerator door. "I don't see how Julian being here makes us any more safe and secure." Opening the breadbox, she pulled out the loaf of honey wheat she baked. "Yes," she chuckled. "He knows I have a gun, and it's probably his safety he should be concerned about. Stop making me laugh. I'm mad at you." She pulled a bread knife from the block. "All right, I'll see you when you get home. I love you too, but I'm still mad."

She hung up the phone, turning back to the window. "Lord, please give me strength," she sighed. His T-shirt dangled from the back pocket of the jeans riding low on his slim hips. Sweat was already beading up on the tan skin of his wide shoulders and back, the roped muscles of his arms jumping and bunching as he carried a plank to the sawhorses he set up. The buzz saw screamed as he flicked a switch, and began cutting smaller planks.

She was mesmerized, the sight of him bringing back such cherished memories. Memories of the boy who stole her heart before she was old enough to understand what that meant, the young man who swore they were born to be together …

And the man who walked away, leaving her with nothing but memories as a reminder she just wasn't enough for Julian Montgomery.

Chapter Four

*B*y the time Julian showered the sawdust and sweat from his body, Rowan had the entire house smelling like heaven. He entered the kitchen to find her rolling out piecrust. The chicken stewing on the stove could only mean pot pie. His mouth watered as he grabbed a beer from the fridge, and straddled a stool at the island to watch her. Peas and carrots had already been chopped, along with a pile of the herbs she harvested all summer. When she pulled the lid off the pot to lift the chicken out to cool so she could debone it, his eyes nearly rolled back in his head.

His gaze skimmed over the snug-fitting T-shirt hugging her breasts and the even snugger jeans with holes in the knees. Her face, flushed from the steam rising up from the pot, was scrubbed clean, her dark curls pinned into a messy knot atop her head. Between running a business and catering to those she loved, Rowan rarely made time for primping and preening. Yet there was something undeniably sexy, even sultry about her as she moved around the kitchen where she was most happy. His blood stirred hotly as he took a long draw of his beer.

"You remember the first time you made me a pot pie?" he asked as he caught a glimpse of her smooth, firm belly when she reached up into a cabinet for a bowl. His fingers tightened around the beer bottle.

"Mm-hmm." She pulled tender hunks of chicken from bones. "You said it wasn't as good as Millie's," she recalled with a tight smile.

"No," he said quickly. "I said it was almost as good as Millie's."

"Same thing." She spooned a bit of the broth into a skillet with flour and milk to stir up gravy.

"I was a stupid fifteen year old boy, Rowan," he chuckled.

"Yes, I recall that as well." Turning her attention back to her task, she ignored him once more. Going to the bay of windows in the breakfast nook, he surveyed the backyard and the bank of the lake. "They're out there, Julian."

He turned in time to see her bend over to slide the pie into the oven. Fire licked along his veins as he raised the beer to his lips.

"Ryan has uniforms surrounding us. I'm betting Ava drops by every hour or so to prod them into standing at attention. My home is officially an armed fortress," she said. The door of the oven slapped shut.

"I know this is difficult for you." Setting his beer on the island, he reached for her.

She lifted the mixing spoon she held in a hand. "No! You have no idea," she snapped. "I knew you'd be back, but right here … every time I turn around." She shook her head, turning her back to him as they heard the front door open and close.

"Hi, honey! I'm home!"

Daisy Covington burst into the kitchen, dragging a rolling suitcase behind her, and toting a purse almost as big over one shoulder. Her dark, glossy hair was clipped into a stylish pixie accentuating her almond-shaped brown eyes and the bone structure women would die for. Tall and lithe, she wore a black suede vest that laced up her back, a short floral skirt that swirled around her slim thighs, and a pair of black leather combat boots. She dropped the handle of the suitcase, tossed the vibrant red purse onto the island, and slapped her hands to her hips.

"Julian," she said with a pretty pout. "I'm waiting."

He grinned and caught her up into a hug that left her boots dangling around his knees. "Shame on you, Daisy," he chuckled against her cheek. "You went and turned into a beautiful woman while I was looking the other way."

She crinkled her nose, jabbing an elbow into his ribs as he set her back on her feet. "Yeah, and I know which way you were looking," she drawled. Turning to her sister, she pointed a finger. "Cry and I will use it against you."

Rowan blinked back tears, lifted her arms, and her baby sister stepped into them. "It's been more than a year," she whispered. "I know Europe needs good forensic anthropologists, but how we have missed you." Holding her sister at arm's length, she sniffed back more tears.

Julian recognized the look passing between them, the look between siblings that said more than words. The same look he shared with his brothers, and Zane and Ava shared when they weren't all brawling. It was the soundless communication between those who came from the same place, the ones who shared their entire lives.

"Good forensic anthropologist?" Daisy raised a brow. "Sis, I am one of the best," she insisted with a wink in Julian's direction.

"There's the humility you are so well known for," Rowan chuckled.

"Where's Mama?" Daisy snatched a chunk of carrot from the island.

"She should be home from the shop any minute now." Rowan reached for a potholder. "There's a chicken pot pie in the oven, but you've got time. Give him a kiss for me while you're at it."

"Will do." Daisy turned on a heel, and went down the hallway. "Julian, you eat all that pie, and you're in big trouble!" she called over a shoulder.

"Well, looks like the gang is all here," Rowan murmured, cracking the oven door to peek at the pie.

"Yeah." Julian slid back onto a stool. "I don't remember the last time we were all home at the same time."

"Daddy's funeral." She closed the oven, tossing the pot holder aside. "Since then either Daisy was home, and you weren't. Ava was here, but one of you wasn't. The old folks might not be able to stand it." Tears welled in her eyes again, and the panic seized him. "I'm glad," she whispered. "I didn't want the next time we were all together to be another funeral. As horrible as the circumstances are, I'm so glad you're all home."

She didn't resist when he reached for her this time. Maybe because this time they were two people who loved the same people—and as happy to be together as they were fearful of what that might mean for all of them.

•

Aiden heard his mother greet her in the foyer. Ava treated him to breakfast at the Waffle House that morning, and now Daisy. She swept into his study looking so much like Millie the day Remy married her he could hardly believe his old eyes. Rowan favored her mother too, but she had Remy's quiet confidence and gentle nature … except when his boy got her riled, of course. Daisy was her mama through and through, just as Ava could never deny she belonged to Flo. What wonderful reminders they all were of the lives and love he and their parents shared since they were just kids roaming the backwoods and water's edge of Crystal Lake.

He opened his arms, and she fell into them. He saw the shock and despair as her eyes roamed his face, knew how she mourned the disease that had robbed him, and would take the ultimate toll on them all.

"Now listen to me, girl," he said as she tried hard not to cry. "Like I told Ava, you, Julian and she needed to go out and make your way in the world. I wouldn't have it any other way."

She nodded, hugging him to her tightly.

"I'm proud of all you've accomplished, Daisy." He cupped her face in his hands. "Your daddy would be too." He kissed her cheek. "We'll visit more tomorrow. Right now, I think your mama could probably use your help keeping your sister from skinning my boy alive."

"You're probably right about that." She stood, swiping tears from her cheeks. "I'll have Rowan cook us pancakes for breakfast. She'll owe me by then." She dropped another kiss on his pale cheek.

"Daisy?" She stopped in the doorway, and turned. "Stay close to your sister. And see what you can do to help the others stop this madness."

"Rowan will be fine," she assured. "And God help the fool who tries to cross all of us."

•

Julian sat on the back porch, admiring his handiwork in the moonbeams slanting across the steps. He made rounds, checking in with all the officers stationed across the seven acres butting up to the water. It gave him a chance to walk off the half a chicken pot pie he inhaled. After eating in fast food restaurants and dives for months, home cooking was sheer heaven. Not to mention having a front row seat to Rowan, Daisy and Millie catching up. It was good to see Rowan laugh again. He hadn't forgotten what a breathtaking sight that could be.

"It must be hell being you, Julian."

Ryan rounded the porch, taking the steps two at a time. He traded his uniform for jeans and a UT T-shirt, but Julian knew his firearm was still tucked into his waistband, and he'd left strict instructions he was to be called if anything suspicious occurred. His brother might be a smartass skirt-chaser, but he was as good a sheriff as their old man once was.

"Gran said Daisy is home." Ryan peered through the screen door.

"Yeah," Julian confirmed. "She's acting like she's just here for an ordinary visit, but I'm betting she's anxious to go over the autopsy reports."

"I'll have them to her first thing in the morning." Ryan stepped back as the screen door swung open. "Damn, Daisy!" he grunted as she stepped out onto the porch into his arms. "When did you grow up so good?"

"Well," she corrected, placing a kiss on his cheek. "Did y'all think I would stay sixteen forever?"

"I personally have been a fan of you being legal for a while now," Ryan said with a leer. "Now that you are, go get your sister. I hear there's a welcome home party for you, Ava, and the twin not nearly as handsome as me down at the roadhouse."

"Yee-haw," Daisy drawled, pulling the screen door open. "Rowan! Party at the roadhouse! Let's go!" The screen slapped closed behind her.

"You know it will take half an hour for them to decide what to wear," Julian said.

His brother sat down on the porch steps. "I know."

"Then another half hour for Rowan to try to talk Daisy out of what she decides on."

Ryan looked up at the stars dotting the heavens. "Dear Lord, please let Daisy win this one."

•

Rowan sat in the large booth at the roadhouse, sipping a glass of the Riesling Flo kept chilled just for her. Ava and Daisy were at a pool table teaching Zane and Ryan a lesson in humility as well as giving the good ol' boys of Crystal Lake something to dream about. Ava apparently painted on the jeans she wore, and swiped a tight-fitting tank top from her mama's stash. Daisy finally relented after much browbeating from her big sister, agreeing to wear a camisole under the sheer black blouse that wasn't much more than a scarf. She had to lie on the floor and wiggle into the black leather skirt while Rowan tugged on the zipper. The hem of the skirt barely skimmed the tops of the red suede thigh high boots she snatched up in Paris.

Rowan knew the royal blue knit dress clinging to her curves was a good choice when her sister didn't roll her eyes and make gagging noises. She blew the dust off a pair of nude heels that gave the illusion of the long legs she wasn't born with, and left her riot of curls loose. For Rowan, letting her hair down was a definite statement of intent. As her evenings were typically spent trying to balance the budget for the flower shop or curled up with a good book, soaking up the ambiance of the roadhouse on a Friday night was a rare treat indeed.

Her view of the pool table was blocked as he slid into the booth beside her. He set another glass of Riesling before her as he sipped his frosty draft. "It's been a long time since you tried to get me drunk, Julian." Draining the glass in her hand, she set it aside.

"As I recall the last time I did so, we ended up on Ryan's boat out in the middle of the lake under a full moon," he whispered in her ear.

She smiled, more touched than he would ever know by how accurate he was. When she turned her head, he was right there. His tawny eyes glinted with the same heat spiraling through her, his mouth so close she could almost taste his kiss. "Bygones and all that," she murmured, lifting the wineglass to her lips. His cocky smile faded as the color drained from his face.

"Hey, Logan."

Julian turned to scowl at his brother as he slid into the booth across from them.

"Hey, gorgeous," Logan greeted. Signaling the cocktail waitress at the bar, he glanced at Julian. "What?"

"Nothing," his brother grunted as he lifted his beer to drain half the mug.

"Hi, Sherry." Logan gave the waitress the sly grin that sent every single woman in Crystal Lake swooning. "I would love a draft, the potato skins, pulled pork nachos, and the fried green tomatoes." He looked back and forth between Julian and Rowan. "Y'all want anything?" When they shook their heads, he shot Sherry another mind-numbing smile. "That's all, sweetheart. Thanks!" he called after her as he watched her wriggle back toward the bar. His gaze shifted to the pool tables. "Wow! Who is the honey shooting a combo?"

Rowan leaned forward in order to see past Julian. Her eyes flicked back to Logan. "The honey is my little sister."

Logan's eyes rounded. "Are you kidding me?" He craned his neck to see around Sherry as she set the beer before him. "Good God, Rowan, couldn't you at least put some clothes on her before you let her out of the house?" He looked at his brother. "Is she old enough to be in here?"

"She's almost twenty-six," Rowan chuckled. "And I did the best I could with her wardrobe." She raised her glass with a heavy sigh.

"She can't be anywhere near twenty-six," Logan muttered, watching Daisy lean over the table to make another shot. His eyes bugged out again. "Isn't she a lot younger than me?"

"Three years," Julian reminded. "Though that's a lot when she's sixteen and you aren't."

Logan frowned as he watched Zane all but trip over his own tongue. "Somebody needs to do something," he grumbled as he slid out of the booth. "Before she and Ava start a riot in here."

Rowan watched him stride to the pool tables with a knowing smile. "Well, well," she mused as she watched her sister jump into Logan's arms. "I give Flo two minutes before she has your father and my mother on the line."

Julian shifted in the seat, blocking her view. "Why don't you finish your wine?" he suggested with a slow smile. Leaning closer, he trailed a fingertip along her cheek. "Then maybe we could take a drive out by the lake." When she lifted a brow, he rolled his eyes. "Fine," he gritted out. "But we both know it's still there, Rowan."

"It?" She set down her glass, intentionally averting her gaze. He laid a finger under her chin, forcing her to meet his eyes.

"You know exactly what I'm talking about. Are you going to lie to me, and tell me I'm wrong?"

She was challenging his pride. That never had set well with him. But, she had her own pride to haggle with, and she wasn't about to let too much wine and his sharply honed prowess make a fool out of her again.

"We're adults, Julian," she reminded coolly. "As adults we should have enough sense not to act on every impulse—"

"Impulse?" he snapped. His eyes narrowed into glistening slits of amber as he moved so close she was plastered up against the back of the booth. "Are you serious, Rowan?" Apparently it was a rhetorical question, as he didn't seem interested in waiting for a response. "An impulse is buying a candy bar, or lottery ticket. Deciding to turn left instead of right, or do I want fries with that. An impulse doesn't follow you around … for years! It doesn't wake you up in the middle of the night, or worse yet make sleeping at all impossible. An impulse doesn't make everything else pale in comparison, leaving you wondering what the hell you were thinking trying to drown memories in somebody who doesn't hold a candle to … What?" he snarled as Ryan tapped on his shoulder again.

"We have to go," his brother insisted. "Right now, Julian!"

•

Julian told Rowan to wait in the truck. It was apparently a complete waste of breath.

The charming ranch-style house less than a mile from the downtown square looked much like all the others crowding the middleclass neighborhood where kids still played kick the can under streetlights. Dogs barked as sirens wailed, front porch lights flicking on as people emerged from their homes to mill around the crime scene tape a uniform was stringing across the lawn. Julian knew by the expression the first responders wore as they exited the house the scene inside wasn't one they would soon forget. Grabbing Rowan's hand, he tugged her along behind him as he followed his brothers inside.

Daisy knelt over the butchered body of a young woman, and Ava hovered over her shoulder as they both pulled on latex gloves. Ryan pulled a pair out of his pocket as Logan swiped a hand over his face with a frustrated groan. When Julian felt Rowan's fingers tighten around his, he turned to find her staring down at the white tulip in the cold hand of a woman who looked remarkably like her. Curling an arm around her slumped shoulders, he looked at his brother.

"Come on, honey," Logan whispered, pulling Rowan to his side. "Let's let them do their jobs." He nodded at Julian as he guided her back toward the door. "We'll be at her place."

"Thanks, little brother," Julian mumbled, wondering if he would ever forget the horrified expression on Rowan's face. Forcing his attention back to the victim, he did his best to shove all personal issues aside. Obviously the others were attempting to do the same.

Ryan rifled through a purse on the sofa, pulling out a wallet. "Shannon Peterson, twenty-nine years old. Cash and credit cards still here, so robbery apparently not a motive." He glanced at a uniform coming down a narrow hallway, shaking his head. "She lives alone."

Daisy carefully lifted the lapel of a jacket from the victim's chest. "Cause of death most likely a single stab to the heart, further verification of this to be determined at the time of autopsy." Her gaze scanned the woman's body. "I note fifteen other stab wounds, also to be cataloged at the time of autopsy." Lifting one of the woman's hands, she studied her nails. "It does not appear the victim struggled with her attacker. Angle of the wound to the chest suggests she was stabbed from behind, as a result likely taken by surprise. Lack of blood flow to other wounds suggests they were inflicted postmortem." Pulling off the gloves, she looked up at Ryan. "I'd like to attend the autopsy if you can get the coroner to sign off on it."

"Absolutely," he replied with a nod.

"Julian and me, too," Ava added as she scribbled notes onto a pad.

Ryan stepped closer to his twin. "You okay?" he whispered as more people crowded into the room.

"Fine." Julian stared at the woman who only hours ago had the rest of her life to look forward to. "Who found her?"

"A friend stopped by to drop off some cookie dough she bought from a school fundraiser. They agreed on a time for her to drop it off, so when she didn't answer the door and the friend saw her car in the drive, she called it in. She's outside, but my boys already have her statement."

Julian's eyes skipped over the tidy living room. Not so much as a throw pillow out of place. He frowned, turning back to his brother. "Which school?"

"What?" Ryan stepped back as the coroner rushed in, and knelt beside the victim.

"Which school was the fundraiser for?"

Ryan flipped open a pad. "The high school basketball team. The cookie dough is a big seller. Gran always buys—"

"Are names and addresses listed on the order forms?"

"Yeah, I think so," Ryan replied as they watched the body being lifted onto a gurney.

"Many of the folks who support the team would also attend the games," Julian mused. Spotting a sofa table lined with photos, he skirted the crowd.

Ryan followed, stopping at his side as he scanned the pictures. Lifting a photo of a teenage boy in a Crystal Lake High basketball uniform, he handed it to his brother. "Find out who this kid is. Maybe the other victims are Indians fans as well."

•

Julian found her on the back porch, watching the moonlight glimmer on the water like millions of tiny gemstones cast between the muddy banks. A uniformed officer disappeared around the side of the house as he sat down on the step beside her. Curling an arm around her shoulders, he pulled her to his side.

"I recognized her." Rowan tugged the cardigan closer around her as the breeze picked up. "She came into the shop sometimes. She sent her mother yellow roses for her birthday a couple of months ago." A tear rolled down her cheek as Julian wondered if he'd ever felt more helpless in his life. "I keep thinking what it will be like for her. What would life be like without a daughter who sent yellow roses on your birthday?"

Because he didn't know the answer to her question, but was just as tortured by the thought as she was, he pressed a kiss to her temple. "Do you remember anything else about her?"

She shook her head, leaning into the solid warmth of his body. "She had a sister," she said suddenly. "I remember she put her name on the card with the flowers. She said her sister had three kids, so she always put her name on them. We laughed about how having three kids might cause you to forget your own name, not to mention birthdays."

"That's good." He dropped another kiss on the top of her head. "That will help."

"Three kids would be nice," she said with a sniff. "Two boys and a girl."

"Why not two girls and a boy?" he mumbled against her cheek.

"Because two sisters would make his life a nightmare," she

chuckled.

"I suppose you're right," he said with a soft smile. "Though I can assure you, brothers are no picnic."

She looked at him through the thin wash of moonlight. "You have to stop this, Julian, even if it means making me an easier target."

"You know there is no way I will—"

"If using me as bait means this nightmare can be over, you'll do exactly that." She stood, hesitating as he curled a hand around the back of her thigh. Her hand fell to glide through his hair. "I'm not nearly as scared as you are. Seeing you and all the others this way is exactly what this maniac wants. End it, Julian, so we can all get on with our lives."

•

"No way!" Ryan crossed his arms over his chest with a shake of his head. Squinting against the morning sunlight pouring into the kitchen window, he glanced at his twin. "I argued the necessity of funding round the clock protection for this place until I was blue in the face. Now you want me to call it off?"

"We'll all be here," Logan reminded. "I might not have a badge, but I'm as good a shot as you."

"You are not!" Ryan barked.

"I'm a better shot than any of you," Ava bragged, slitting open one of the biscuits that had just come out of the oven. When Rowan lifted a brow as she set a platter of eggs on the harvest table, she shrugged. "Fine, you're the best shot."

"She is not!" Daisy balked, licking peach preserves off a spoon. "Last time we shot cans off stumps, I blew every one of you away." Julian poured another mug of coffee. "The point is we all know how to handle a firearm." He set the pot on a trivet on the table. "As much as I dislike the idea, Rowan is right. The killer is more likely to start skulking around here, and hopefully not stalking other victims, if uniforms aren't scattered every five feet along the property."

"Ryan, I appreciate your concern." Rowan laid a hand on his shoulder as he sat down at the table. Once the rest were seated, she sat, and began passing bacon, grits, eggs and biscuits. "I'm not good at being held prisoner. Millie doesn't want me at the shop for fear of not only risk to me, but possibly customers. I worry about her and Daisy being here with me if God forbid ..." Her eyes met

Julian's. "We can send Millie to stay with Aiden and Gran. Ryan, you could post some uniforms there to make us all rest a bit easier."

He shoved a strip of bacon into his mouth as he nodded. "Zane staying at your folks' place?" he directed at Ava.

"Yep. Mama is loving it. She'll have him reverted back to the age of ten soon. Not that he's progressed much further than that being out on his own," Ava drawled as she passed the biscuits.

"I'm thinking how much the old man will love having Gran and Millie fussing over him," Julian chuckled as he plopped grits onto his plate.

"Then it's settled." Logan lifted a forkful of eggs. "We all hunker down here, and see if we can reel in a murderer."

"Oh, goody," Daisy said with a wide smile. "I love sleepovers!"

Chapter Five

$\mathcal{I}$t had been less than twenty-four hours, and the sleepover was already grating on Rowan's last nerve. She didn't even have going to work to look forward to. Ava insisted on sleeping in her bedroom. She woke up twice during the night to find her friend nervously pacing, and muttering to herself under her breath. There was always a line for the bathroom, and Julian and his brothers were constantly arguing over every little thing.

The dining room had been converted into command central. The files Logan had released were spread all over the table as they sorted through them in hopes of coming up with anything that might be relevant. Daisy studied the photos of the victims over and over, along with the autopsy reports. She confirmed the coroner's conclusion the murders were perpetrated by the same attacker, using the same weapon. Julian and Ava combed through files, trying to jog each other's memory about this case, or that one. Ryan kept in touch with Zane and the officers he posted at the flower shop and his father's place through the radio always clutched in his hand. Logan scribbled notes as they went through the information and batted around ideas it might bring to mind.

They all looked up from their assigned chores as Rowan set a tray of glasses of iced tea and thick sandwiches in the center of the table. "Eat," she ordered, slapping closed the file before Ava. Daisy laid a hand over the autopsy reports before she could whisk them away. "Since I know none of you will be swayed, why don't you tell me what you've come up with so far?" She pulled a chair up by her sister's.

"Nothing that makes any sense yet," Julian sighed as he reached for a ham and cheese and a glass of tea. "I'm beginning to wonder if all this is a waste of time."

"Maybe not," Logan mumbled around a big bite of turkey on rye. He sifted through pages of a thick file before him. "Julian, do you remember a perp named Ronald Massey?"

Julian leaned back in his chair, his brow creasing with a frown. "Yeah. He was an informer in a meth lab ring in Virginia several years back." His eyes locked with Ava's. "I was brought in to go undercover after a DEA agent went missing."

"I was brought in when the agent's body was recovered along with three others who were known associates of the ring," Ava said. "Massey was busted after a raid on his trailer produced a lab he was operating for the ring." She shook her head. "He was cooking that poison with his girlfriend and kid right there to breathe every noxious fume. Julian was the one who got him and the girlfriend to roll over in exchange for a lighter sentence."

Logan ripped a report from the file. "Ronald was jumped in the shower at the state pen six months later." His eyes scanned the report. "He was killed by a fellow inmate. Sixteen wounds in total, but it was a stab to the heart that was determined to be the cause of death."

An eerie silence settled around the room. Rowan set down her glass. "I assume that is the sort of clue you've been hoping for."

Julian stood, going to the windows with a sweeping view of the lush countryside. "It does answer a lot of questions. An eye for an eye." He turned to Ava. "You were right."

"Unfortunately I usually am," she murmured, scanning the report in Logan's hand. "Whoever murdered those women sees it as retribution. If I had to bet—"

"The girlfriend," Ryan insisted, looking over Logan's other shoulder. "Marie Cox. She had a long list of priors at the time of her and Massey's arrests for the lab operation. Check forgery, petty drug pedaling, and a couple of assaults on officers."

"She sounds charming." Daisy set the sandwich she hadn't touched back on the platter. "What happened to the kid?"

Logan sifted through the file. "He was turned over to DCS. As he was a minor, any records about that would be sealed."

"See if you can get a judge's order to unseal them," Julian instructed. "And request all state and federal files on this Marie Cox." He turned back to the windows. "I'm betting she's served her time for the drug charges, and has decided to settle some old scores in Crystal Lake."

•

Rowan ran everybody out of the kitchen after supper, insisting she would rather tackle the mess alone. His brothers were still holed up in the dining room, making calls and going over all they'd sketched out so far. Ava was updating their superiors, assuring they still had the situation under control. Daisy, still battling jetlag, decided to call it an early night.

Julian sat on the back porch, his gaze constantly scanning as far as he could see. Thick forest surrounded the house all the way to the water's edge. Taking cover there wouldn't be difficult until the place quieted for the night. He wouldn't be able to explain it to anyone else, but he had a feeling things were fine for now. He often had a sixth sense about these kinds of things that was invaluable in his undercover work. He'd long ago learned when the hair on the back of his neck stood up to pay attention, no matter how unreasonable it might seem to others.

She stepped out onto the porch with a steaming mug in each hand. He took the one she offered as Rowan settled into the rocker by his. "The last of the meatloaf is hidden in the bottom drawer in the fridge," she confided as she lifted the coffee to her lips. "Though if you don't get back to it by midnight, I'm sure Ryan will have already sniffed it out."

"You're probably right," he chuckled. "What about the last piece of apple pie?"

She smiled. "Daisy took it up with her."

"Damn," he muttered into his cup. "As I haven't seen her eat more than a bite or two since she got here, I suppose I won't offer to arm wrestle her for it."

"I'll make another tomorrow. It's not like I have anything else to do." Her voice was tight with the frustration she'd been choking on for days.

"I know this has been rough on you." He watched moonlight streak along her glossy curls and glint in her dark eyes. "I'm sorry you're paying for what Ava and I did."

"You did your jobs, Julian." She stared down into her mug. "And I owe you an apology."

"Good," he drawled with a grin. "For what?"

"I accused you of being a shiftless gambler turning your back on your family for no good reason." Her eyes met his in the frothy light. "Why didn't you tell me?"

He wanted to tell her. He could recall dozens of times he wanted her to know he wasn't the shameless, self-centered jerk he appeared to be. Especially since he knew if there was anybody else in the world who knew him heart and soul, it was Rowan. She thought he was just lost. The truth was he found the best part of himself doing the work few others could stomach.

"I didn't tell you for the same reason I didn't tell the others." He let his eyes sweep the yard again, settled his gaze on the brightly colored mums waving in the breeze. "I didn't want you to worry."

"So instead you let me think ..." She trailed off as he pushed up onto his feet.

"Better that than you worrying all the time." He stood at the railing, watching the wind stir the water now. "I kept thinking once I got it out of my system ..." He drew a deep breath. "But, then there was always another case. When I did come back, you made it abundantly clear you didn't want to see me." He turned to face her. "I know this is the only place for you. But, there is a whole world out there, Rowan."

She stood, and came to his side. "Tell me about it."

"What do you mean?" She perched on the railing, and he stepped between her thighs to keep her anchored in place. When she didn't resist, he laid his palms to her thighs, glided them up along her hips.

"I mean," she said with a smile as he looped his arms around her waist. "Tell me about all the things you've seen, the places you've been, and the people you've met."

"That could take a while." His lips skimmed her forehead as he breathed the scent of her skin and hair. All the fear and frustration he'd been stuffing deep down inside eased for the first time since this whole mess began.

"I've got a while." She circled his neck with her arms. "And Julian not once in my entire life have I not wanted to see you. It was seeing you, and knowing you'd be leaving again I couldn't take." He nodded, and then laid his forehead to hers. "Now tell me," she encouraged. "Start with New Orleans. I've always wanted to go there."

•

Ava peered through the screen, a smile creeping across her face. She watched Julian scoop Rowan from the railing, and settle her on his lap as he sat in the rocker. Their voices were lower now, so she couldn't make out what they were saying, but she figured not screaming at each other at the top of their lungs was good progress. When she turned, she jumped, a hand flying to her chest as her heart skipped a few beats.

"Ryan!" she hissed, swatting at his shoulder. "You scared the snot out of me!"

"What are you doing?" he mumbled around a mouthful of meatloaf.

"Nothing," she said quickly. He stepped around her, peering out the door. He cocked a brow as he turned back to her. "I was just making sure they weren't brawling."

He glanced back out the door. "No worries there." Stepping around her, he went to the fridge to pull out a carton of milk.

Ava sat on a stool at the island. "My superiors have agreed to continue letting us handle things here."

"Good." Ryan straddled another stool as he splashed milk into a glass. "I'd hate to have to start shooting to clear my office of feds in fancy suits."

"Everything on file regarding Marie Cox and Massey is being sent to us pronto." She dropped her chin into a hand. "I have a feeling it's still going to be a matter of waiting for her to make another move."

"Me too." He swiped milk from his lips with a napkin, then crumpled it in a hand. "I also have a feeling it won't be long. She has our full attention now. That's what she's been waiting for."

Ava looked out the screen door again. "She better hope we catch her before she can cause Rowan any harm. I don't even like to think about what Julian would do if we don't."

Ryan drew a deep breath, and then reached across the island to lay a hand over hers. When her eyes met his, they both just stared for a moment. "We'll stop her, Ava," he assured lowly. Her fingers tightened around his just before he drew them away. "Then you and my brother can get back to saving the rest of the world."

His footsteps echoed in the hallway as he left her in the quiet kitchen to stare after him.

•

Rowan led the way up the stairs, down the hallway to her bedroom. She could hear Ava and Daisy in her sister's room, and Logan and Ryan in one of the two guest rooms. Undoubtedly they all still had their heads together mulling over the case, or perhaps just looking for ways to make the time pass as they waited like sitting ducks. She stopped outside her door, and turned. Julian untangled their fingers, lifting his hand to strum it through her curls.

"You're not going to invite me in are you?" His eyes roamed her face, his hand cupping the back of her neck to gently knead the muscles there.

"No, I'm not." She laid a palm to his chest, felt the steady, strong beat of the heart that had called to hers for as long as she could remember. "I understand now. I know being here wasn't right for you, and now I know why. But, nothing has changed, Julian."

"Rowan," he sighed, pulling her closer.

"Listen to me." She pressed a fingertip to his lips. "I paid very close attention. I saw your face as you spoke of a job you love. Even when you talked about the terrible things you've seen, I could see in your eyes how much it means to you to do something about it. Your life outside of Crystal Lake means every bit as much to you as mine here means to me. It wasn't fair for me to think if you didn't want the life I did, you were wrong. I'm sorry for that."

"I don't want an apology." He framed her face in his hands. "The only thing I want you to understand is no matter where I go, or what I do, it never goes away. I think of you, and God knows every time I see you … I'm that same kid again. The one who would swim the lake to get to you, or give just about anything for one more kiss out on the front porch."

"Sometimes I'm still that girl too," she admitted as her heart wrenched with his confession. "But, most of the time I am a grown woman, who understands how we feel about each other doesn't change what we need. I'm all for the romantic notion love conquers all, but we both know in reality it doesn't."

"What if I stayed?" he suggested quickly. Bringing her mouth to his, he kissed her, a hungry, hard kiss that had her sagging against him.

Wrapping her fingers around his wrists, she pulled his hands from her face as she eased back. "You're not being fair," she gasped as her brain and body waged war.

He heaved out a breath as he shoved his hands into his pockets. "What do you want from me?" he groaned. "God, Rowan, I'm damned if I do, damned if I don't with you."

"I want you to not say things you don't mean just to get into my bed," she said tightly. "I'm not some diversion on the road happy to take a tumble, and then watch your taillights fade out of sight until the next time you come my way."

She was trembling now with the fury fate could have dealt them this hand. She hadn't asked him to tell her about his life to know more about the thrills and chills of a federal agent. She asked because she needed to know for sure. She wanted to see for herself, and she had. It was who he was. And Julian couldn't be who he was here anymore than she could be who she was away from here.

He paced up and down the hallway for a moment before stopping to press his back against the wall. "Just so I'm clear, you're telling me if I stayed, it still wouldn't change anything between us?" He lifted a hand as her mouth popped open. "And don't you ever compare what I feel for you with—" He scrubbed his hand over his chin. "I want to try, Rowan. Just tell me what I have to do."

She stared at him for a silent moment that seemed as long as the years that led them to this one. "You have to stop being who you are, Julian. Or I have to stop being who I am. When you figure out how either of us can do that, let me know." Stepping into her bedroom, she quietly closed the door behind her.

•

From the steep rise above the water she could see the house, and the sprawl of lawn reaching the banks. They called off their dogs, not a single cop standing guard on the property, or milling around the house. With the exception of the feds and the sheriff inside, waiting for her next move.

She smiled, the sense of satisfaction warming her as the cold wind rustled the limbs of trees, and spun fallen leaves into multicolored swirls around her. Doing time allowed her to rid her body of the drugs that clouded her mind since she was just a kid, helped her to focus and plan. Seven years locked away, knowing the only one who mattered died in a pool of blood in a stinking hole where he was supposed to be protected. The only reason her fate hadn't been the same was a warden who didn't want too much attention on the hellhole she ran stashed her in solitary the minute she heard about the stabbing.

Years of lonely confinement, searching for ways to keep what little sanity she had left. And she'd found the perfect way. She plotted and planned until the days ran together in a litany of revenge and restitution. By the time those bars swung open, she knew exactly what steps to take to lead her to this moment. Now she need only be patient a little longer, be sure not to tip her hand until every last piece of the puzzle was in place. Casting one last glance at the dark, quiet house, she pulled the sleeping bag up around her as she lie back on the hard ground.

Sleeping alone in the cold was nothing new, but watching stars twinkle overhead was. Once she evened the score, they would head some place warmer. Maybe Mexico … She chuckled, thinking warm nights wouldn't be the only reason that would be advisable. Running for the rest of her life, or even paying the ultimate price would be worth it. She made a promise. Unlike the lying feds who used them up to get what they wanted, and then tossed them into hell, she kept her word.

"I'll make it right, baby," she whispered to the night. "When I do, maybe we can both finally rest."

•

Julian tossed another log up onto the stump, his breath forming a cloud around his face as the morning breeze blew in an unusually early frost. Lifting the axe, he brought it down with a swift, accurate swing. The log split, the pieces tumbling off the stump. He tossed them into the messy pile as he caught sight of his twin leaning against a tall pine.

Ryan took another bite of the cinnamon roll as he eyed the pile of wood. "Either you're expecting a blizzard," he mumbled around the roll. "Or she has royally pissed you off." When Julian only dropped another log onto the stump, he licked frosting off his fingertips. "I remember junior year in high school when she told you she was thinking about the University of South Carolina, rather than UT." He began stacking the logs into a neater pile. "You damn near busted a gut. Said it was crazy to leave home when there was a perfectly good university forty minutes down the road. She said you could go with her." He glanced up at his brother as he reached for two more logs. "You said you weren't going anywhere. And neither was Rowan."

Julian brought the axe down again. The blade drove into the stump. Using the tail of the flannel shirt he wore to mop sweat from his brow, he watched the fog hovering over the lake roll back as sunlight exploded through the trees. "She didn't go," he murmured.

"No, she didn't." Ryan kept adding to the pile. "I think that was Rowan's window. I figure we all have them. Mine was after I graduated from the academy." He looked at his twin over a shoulder. "About the same time as yours opened. I thought about it. I even checked into openings on the force in Nashville and Atlanta. I wasn't sure staying around here to spend the rest of my life being Aiden Montgomery's boy was all I wanted out of it." He dusted bark and grit from his hands as he turned to face his brother. "Then it occurred to me being Aiden Montgomery's boy was a good start on being the sort of man I wanted to be. I thought of a lot of things that were a whole lot worse than living in his shadow."

"It's not about that anymore." Julian yanked the axe from the stump, tossed it aside, and sat to drop his head into his hands. Furrowing his fingers through his hair, he looked out over the lake again. "If she had asked even once in the last few years, I would have stayed. I all but begged her to last night, and she still didn't. She said I couldn't stop being who I am." He shook his head. "Half the time I don't even know who that is. I wake up in motel rooms not knowing what day it is, sometimes beside a woman whose name I don't even know." He squinted against the sunlight as it crept around them. "There are undercover agents called lifers, those who have been in it so long they have no reason to ever go back. They've turned their backs on family and friends in order to keep them safe, left behind everything in order to do the job. It steals your soul, Ryan."

His brother moved closer, slapped a hand to his shoulder. "Maybe it's time you start looking for a window. Not for Rowan, or even the old man. None of us want anything other than what's best for you. But, you're the only one who can figure that out. Until you do, trying to be what anybody else needs will just keep us all spinning in circles." He trudged up the hill, leaving his twin to watch the fog lift as the sunshine reflected on the water.

•

Aiden sat on the screened porch watching Prince tear across the lawn as Millie tossed the tennis ball the dog would run headfirst into a brick wall to chase. Julian's pickup rolled up the driveway, and the dog stopped in its tracks with the ball clutched in its mouth. When his son climbed out, Prince loped to his side as Julian slung an arm around Millie's shoulders. He was assuring her there was nothing to worry about, though they all knew he had no way of knowing what was to be. He opened the door of her car for her, leaning down to brush another kiss on her cheek as Millie slid behind the wheel. Prince's head shot between them, the slobbery ball landing in her lap. They laughed as his son grabbed the ball to hurl it all the way to the bank of the lake. Prince took off, and Julian waved to Millie as her car backed out of the drive.

Aiden waited, sipping the cup of black coffee as he scanned the morning paper. The morphine jumbled his thoughts so he waved his mother away when she tried to deliver his morning dose. He needed to be sharp now, or at least as much as he could be before the pain pulled him so far under he had no choice but dull it, along with his thoughts. When the door leading into the kitchen opened, he set the paper aside.

"Good morning," Aiden said cheerily as his son set his cup of coffee on a table, and leaned down to hug him. He slapped a hand to Julian's back, wondering where all those years went. His sons had gone from being scrawny kids looking for reassurance from a father to grown men offering reassurance of their own.

"Morning, old man." Julian studied him as he sat in the chair a few feet away. "You get any sleep?"

"Apparently more than you," Aiden drawled, noting the shadows under his son's eyes. "First thing I did this morning was look across the water to be sure all of you being under one roof hadn't blown it to kingdom come."

Julian smiled as he reached for his coffee. "Surprisingly we've made pretty good strides. On squirreling out the lunatic, that is."

"So I hear. Logan called earlier to fill me in. He said you should know more about this Marie Cox when other files arrive later today." Aiden slid the reading glasses from his face to rub his eyes with a finger and thumb. "I suppose about now it would be easy for you and Ava to be feeling responsible for the deaths of those women and the fear we all have for Rowan." Julian didn't reply as he watched Prince scamper back and forth across the yard, sniffing here and pawing there. "I'll remind you doing your job isn't the cause, son. This Marie Cox, if she is the one, obviously has a distorted view of reality. You and Ava adopting one too won't help the situation."

"It isn't just that," Julian muttered. "Massey should have been confined to solitary. We told him ..." He shoved a hand through his hair. "I told him if he rolled, he would be kept separate from the population. According to the file, he was already supposed to be out of that shower, and back in his cell before the stabbing occurred."

"Which means a guard was paid off," Aiden replied softly. "As unfortunate as it is, you and I both know it happens. There is nothing you could have done about it then, and certainly not now."

"I keep thinking about what I would do if she got to Rowan. What sort of vengeance I might come up with."

"Would it include taking innocent lives?" Aiden lifted a brow.

"Of course not," Julian sighed, leaning back in the chair as he sipped his coffee.

"Then I think you trying to liken yourself to anyone who finds that acceptable is a waste of your time, son. As is being here, when I'm sure you have things to do across the way there." Aiden looked out over the water. "Julian."

"I see," he assured, bounding from the chair. "Call Ryan!"

•

Julian was across the yard in seconds, diving into the water so cold it took his breath away. He swam, faster and harder than he ever had in his life. By the time he reached the bank, his muscles wept as his legs trembled under him. When he got to the back porch his brothers had the kid pinned to the side of the house. Rowan came rushing out as the boy's face paled to an ashen shade of gray.

"What is going on out here?" she demanded, elbowing Ryan and Logan out of the way. "Alex, are you all right?"

"Yes, ma'am," the boy stammered. "Millie said you weren't feeling well. My grandmother sent ..." He looked at the container he'd dropped still rolling across the porch. "Soup."

"Oh, how thoughtful of her." Rowan turned to retrieve the soup, her eyes rounding when she saw him shivering and dripping all over the porch. "Good Lord, Julian," she gasped. When Daisy and Ava came rushing out onto the porch, she pointed a finger. "You start a hot bath," she ordered her sister. "Ava, grab a blanket from the mudroom." She pressed her palms to Julian's shoulders as she glanced at his brothers over a shoulder. "And y'all leave that boy alone!"

Ryan stepped back as the others disappeared into the house. "Kid, skulking around other people's property uninvited is never a good idea." He bent over to retrieve the soup container. "Doing it around here could get your scrawny butt shot." He removed the lid from the container. "Get out of here. And thank your grandmother," he called after the boy as he scrambled off the porch. "Chicken noodle is my favorite."

Chapter Six

"What in the world were you thinking?" Rowan yanked the flannel shirt over his head as Julian kicked off his sneakers. The bathroom filled with billowing steam as she tossed the soaked shirt aside. He was still shivering, his teeth chattering as she ripped the belt from around his waist.

"Hold on," he stammered as her fingers hovered at the snap of his jeans. "That water was really cold, honey. Give a guy a break."

"Oh, for God's sake," she spat, turning to shut off the taps of the enormous clawfoot tub. "Just get in."

She truly feared his body temperature might have gotten low enough to cause harm. He stepped into the tub, a thankful moan rumbling through his chest as he immersed his body in the steamy water. Kneeling by the tub, she grabbed a sea sponge, and dipped it into the water. Drizzling the warm water over his head, she breathed a sigh of relief as color flooded back into his cheeks.

"Who is that kid?" he finally asked as she continued to dip the sponge, and squeeze water over his head and shoulders.

"He's our delivery boy at the shop. He's a sweet, shy boy who is now probably reevaluating his decision to work for us."

Rolling his head against the back of the tub, he opened one eye as the corners of his lips lifted. "I doubt that. Even after my brothers manhandled him, he still looked at you like an angel come down," he chuckled. "The kid is in love, Rowan." Closing his eyes, he drew another deep breath. "Can't say I blame him."

Dropping the sponge into the water, she scooted back to rest against the vanity. Her heart was still slamming against her chest, her wet hands trembling as she yanked a towel from a bar. "This isn't the time for jokes, Julian."

"I'm not joking." He looked over at her again. "I clearly recall what sort of reaction a boy his age had around you when you were a girl his age. I can only imagine what sort of fuel for the fire the whole older woman aspect adds." His gaze smoothed over her. "You're even more beautiful now."

Her heart lurched again, her knees wobbling as she tried to stand. "Soak for a while. I'll go warm up some of that soup for you."

She was taken completely off guard when his hand shot out, and twisted in the front of her T-shirt. Water sloshed all over the floor as she tumbled into his arms. Her thighs straddled his, her palms slapping against his muscular chest as she gasped and blinked water from her eyes.

"Julian!" she wailed, struggling to sit up.

His hand tangled in the hair at the back of her head, his mouth covering hers before she could spout the scathing remark forming on her lips. Then there was only heat and hunger as he dragged her under a firestorm of feeling. Her fingers shaped the roped muscles of his shoulders, her nails scoring the slick flesh of his chest. His hands shot beneath her T-shirt, molding her lace-covered breasts. A moan echoed on the steamy air. She wasn't sure if it was hers or his, only knew they were both spinning out of control in a tumbling fall toward the molten desire always flaring between them.

When she felt his fingers fumbling with the snap of her jeans, she pulled back, broke the ravenous link of his kiss. He sat up, his arms locking around her to keep her in place. "I never stopped wanting you, Rowan. No matter where I went, or what I did, you were always with me."

Always only lasted as long as it took him to get restless and wander back out of her life. He would keep her safe, hold her as close as she would let him until the danger passed. Then he would leave her to pick up the pieces once more. She tugged his arms from around her, awkwardly rose dripping and shaky from the tub. "I'll make a pan of cornbread to go with the soup," she said as she toweled as much water as she could from her clothes.

"Rowan." He reached for her again, but she stepped aside as she tossed the towel to the floor.

She quickly darted out into the hallway, closing the door behind her before he could come after her. Daisy came up the stairs, her eyes widening as she stopped in the hallway. "Not a word," Rowan mumbled. Her sister simply nodded as she brushed past her, and disappeared into her bedroom.

•

Julian shrugged into a T-shirt, then pulled a V-neck cable knit on over it to ward off the chill still settling in his bones. He wasn't sure what he was expecting, but a complete dismissal wasn't anywhere in the ballpark.

Damn, that woman was stubborn.

Raking his fingers through his damp hair, he stepped out into the hallway. Sunshine poured into the windows in the stairwell. He stopped for a moment, letting the heat of it warm his back. He could hear the others in the dining room as he routed toward the kitchen. She was at the stove, stirring soup. He could smell the cornbread baking in the oven.

"Sit down." Rowan tossed a placemat onto the island. 'The cornbread will be about five more minutes." She poured soup into a bowl, setting it on the placemat. "Be careful. It's really hot."

He rolled his eyes as he reached for the spoon she dug out of a drawer. "Can we skip the pleasantly polite conversation?" he asked irritably.

"Fine." She pulled on an oven mitt. "Sit down, shut up and eat."

Giving him a tight smile, she turned to slide the cast iron skillet out of the oven. He drew up a stool as she cut a thick slab of cornbread, set it on a plate, and grabbed the butter dish from the counter. He was issued a hot cup of coffee to round out the attempt to return his body temperature to normal. He hated to burst her bubble, but it had been hovering way past that since she was squirming around on his lap in the tub.

"Thank you," he mumbled around a bite of the cornbread. She might be stubborn, but the woman knew how to make some fine cornbread. He dipped the spoon into the soup to stir it as steam rose to billow before his face. "Sorry about earlier."

She didn't reply as she finished slicing the rest of the cornbread. The spoon clattered in the bowl as he dropped it.

"Actually, that isn't true," he continued. Her eyes flicked up to meet his. "I'm not sorry, Rowan. And I tell you something else. I'm tired." Planting his palms on the island, he stood, leaning across it. "I am sick and tired of this game we've been playing since we were kids. One time, darlin," he bit out. "If you had so much as hinted at wanting me to stay—"

Her hands slapped to the island as she leaned so close they were almost nose to nose. "Don't you dare, Julian Montgomery," she seethed. "You will not saddle me with your regrets, when I have enough of my own to contend with. We both know pride has always outweighed good sense for each of us. You want to hear me say it? Fine! I wanted you to stay. I've lost count of the number of times over the last eight years I wanted you to be content with the life I wanted. But, you weren't. What I wanted wasn't enough for you, and that's okay, as long as you don't stroll back in here, and try to blame me for it."

"I'm not blaming you." He fell back down onto the stool, wondering how something so clear in his mind one minute could make him feel like an idiot in a stupor the next.

"No?" She dropped wedges of cornbread onto a plate. "Sure sounds like it to me."

He stood, skirting the island to stop in front of her as she pulled the apron from around her waist. "Hello." He offered his hand. "I'm Julian." When she didn't oblige him, he grasped her hand, and shook it. "It's a pleasure to meet you."

She stared up at him. "That cold water obviously damaged a few brain cells."

"If we just met, there is no past for either of us to regret, and no future for us to try to avoid as a result." He grinned as the corners of her lips twitched. "Oh, yes ma'am, I gotcha," he drawled, shaking his head.

"What you've got is more reason for me to believe you're about half crazy," she chuckled, pulling her hand from his.

"What did you say your name was again?" He followed her to the sink, snatching the dishrag before she could reach for it.

"I didn't." She lifted a brow as he began washing the soup pot.

"I'll find out," he sighed, handing off the pot as she grabbed a dishtowel. "And when I do, I'm going to ask you to have supper with me."

"What if I say no?" She dried the pot, setting it aside.

"You won't." He scoured frosting from the pan she baked cinnamon rolls in that morning. It had hardened to something akin to cement.

"What makes you so sure?" She wedged a hip against the counter as she tossed him a brush.

"Well, I'm told I'm a fairly good looking guy with a charming disposition." He glanced at her out of the corner of his eye. "And let's face it, honey, you ain't getting any younger." A chuckle rumbled out of his chest as he dodged the swing of the dish towel.

"Proof you aren't as charming as you've been led to believe," she drawled. She dried the pan he offered as she surveyed him from head to toe. "But, I suppose you are good looking enough. Especially considering how slim pickings are around here for an old maid like me." When he took the dish towel to sling it around her neck and draw her closer, she planted a hand in the center of his chest. "I don't kiss strangers, mister."

He cocked his head to one side, and narrowed a tawny eye. "Tell me your name, and we won't be strangers."

Odd how a silly game he contrived to charm her out of a fit seemed to have his fate hanging in the balance. Those dark gypsy eyes stared into his, and for a moment it was like they were strangers stumbling across one another in clumsy efforts to chase a destiny that always seemed just beyond their grasp. Her fingers curled in the front of his T-shirt. She was going to risk it.

He was going to make her glad she did.

"It's Rowan," she murmured against his lips. "Rowan Covington." Stepping back, she smiled as she offered her hand. His gaze dropped to it as he didn't try to hide his disappointment. "Nice to meet you, Julian."

"Yeah," he muttered with a nod of his head.

She lifted a brow again. "Didn't you have something you wanted to ask?"

"Ahhh." He took her hand, shaking it again as his eyes darted around.

"Supper, Julian," she reminded with a roll of her eyes. "Good Lord, am I going to have to lead you through this? I'm an old maid, remember?" She swatted his shoulder as he laughed. "I don't have time for you to drag your heels."

"Rowan Covington, would you do me the honor of having supper with me?" he asked quickly.

She smiled once more, and his heart flipped over like it did when he was a kid standing on her front porch waiting for a goodnight kiss. "Yes, I will, Julian Montgomery," she whispered. He lifted her hand to his lips, placing a kiss on her fingertips. "But, I will warn you. I rarely kiss on the first date."

Her being able to read his mind never had been much of an asset for him. "Huh," he grunted as she tugged her hand away. "In that case, why don't you share my soup and cornbread? We'll call this our first date, and supper our second."

She chewed her lip as she looked over at his lunch. "Deal," she replied, sliding onto a stool. "Now, why don't you tell me a little about yourself, Julian Montgomery?"

•

It was all business in the dining room that was now command central. Rowan and Julian had been summoned before the soup and cornbread had a chance to cool. Ava's Type A touch was evident in the arrangement of information scribbled onto a dry erase board, or pinned to an accompanying corkboard. Files that had once been scattered across the table were now arranged into neat piles Logan referred to as necessary. At the center of this impressive catalog was a picture Rowan examined closely.

Marie Cox didn't appear to be anymore a serial killer than she was. Her long brown hair hung around a face that was probably once considered pretty before a hard life of drug abuse and God only knew what else marred it. She could be any woman on the street, going unnoticed in a town even as small as Crystal Lake. Rowan was sure after more careful examination she had never laid eyes on the woman. Though there was something about her eyes that seemed vaguely familiar.

"All right," Ryan sighed, nodding at her sister. "Daisy thinks she can provide more to back up Marie Cox being our murderer."

Her sister rounded the table, taking the knife he offered as she tugged Ava to her side. "Marie is five feet eight inches tall, less than a fourth of an inch shorter than Ava. Rowan." She waved a hand, and Rowan went to her side. "Now, all the victims were within an inch of your height." She turned her sister so her back was to Ava, and handed their friend the knife. A chill went up Rowan's spine as she felt the tip of the blade press against her flesh through the thin cotton of her T-shirt. "It takes a good amount of strength to drive a blade through a body with enough force to pierce the heart. For a woman Marie's size, trajectory would make all the difference."

She held Ava's hand clutching the knife up so the others could see. "Height would make a difference in trajectory. We know from details in psychological and physical tests often administered to inmates she's right handed, and that makes a difference as well. You can see from Ava and Rowan," she pointed out as Ava mimicked an attack. "The initial fatal wounds delivered to each victim would be approximately in the same place each time given the heights of the attacker and victims." Daisy shrugged a shoulder. "It's not the sort of scientific proof I could take into court, but for me it's another egg in the Marie-Cox-is-our-killer basket."

Rowan turned to face her sister. "But, regardless of height, can't anyone stab in the same spot?"

"Sure," Daisy said with a nod. "But again, the amount of force it would take to pierce the heart is a determining factor. We can tell something about the attacker by the angle of the wound going into the heart, height being one of those factors." She gave her sister a level look. "I'm not insinuating it's the sort of smoking gun we need, but it is something to be considered."

"My turn." Ryan leaned back in his chair as he looked at the board with Marie's picture pinned to it. "Sweet Marie was released five months ago after serving her time for the drug charge that was reduced as a result of her rolling with Massey on the drug ring. She made the first three weekly appointments with her parole officer in Virginia, and then disappeared into thin air. The PO said warrants have been issued as a result of her parole violation, but the general consensus is after she was sprung, Marie met a dubious squealer's fate at the hands of the drug ring, and her body will eventually show up to prove that assumption." He stabbed a forefinger and thumb into his bleary eyes. "She's either scammed an identity with a steady cash flow, or she has help living on the lam. There is no paper trail to tag her since before she went up to serve her time."

"What about the kid?" Julian asked, glancing around the table.

Logan pulled a file from a stack. "I got a judge to order his records be unsealed." He scanned the file. "Mark Massey, only child of Marie Cox and Ronald Massey. He was nine years old at the time of their arrest. DCS dumped him into the foster system until his maternal great aunt, Emily Wilson, came forward three months later to petition the court for guardianship." He looked up at Julian. "Until four months ago they lived in Norfolk, where Mark made the honor roll at school and Emily worked as a cook at a small hotel restaurant."

"And since that time?" Julian drummed his fingertips against the polished mahogany table.

Logan shook his head. "They too have dropped off the face of the earth. Emily hasn't even cashed her late husband's social security checks."

"So much for wondering who's assisting Marie on the lam," Julian muttered.

"The problem with all of this?" Logan sighed. "Even if Marie Cox walked right up to the front door, we don't have enough to take her in, outside of parole violations. None of what we have so far would hold water in court. Before my boss is going to sign off on an arrest for multiple murders, he's going to insist on a lot more than we have, if we knew where to find her to arrest her."

"We find her, and we can send her back to prison for parole violations until we come up with enough to make the murder charges stick." Ryan stood, his gaze fixed on the picture of Marie. "I'm going to have my force comb every inch of this county, turning over every rock and searching every cranny if it comes to that." His eyes shifted to Rowan. "We're not going to wait for her to hurt anybody else in hopes she'll tip her hand."

Ava curled an arm around Rowan's shoulders. "I could have sworn I smelled apple pie baking earlier."

Rowan smiled weakly. "That you did," she said with a nod.

"I say we be really bad and eat dessert before supper," Daisy suggested, taking her sister's hand to draw her out into the hallway. Ava and Logan followed.

Julian laid a hand to his twin's shoulder before he could join the others. "Did you follow up on the high school basketball team?"

Ryan nodded as he reached for the steno pad he was constantly scribbling on. "The kid in the photo in the last victim's house was her nephew. And two of the other victims did also order cookie dough." He shrugged a shoulder. "As did more than half the county." He frowned as he skimmed some chicken scratch Julian didn't have a prayer of making out. "Wait a minute." Going to a stack of files, he began flipping through them. "The first victim ..." He opened a file. "Amy Vance. She was a part-time substitute teacher at the high school. And the third, Susan Tipton ..." His eyes met his brother's as the file slapped back down onto the table. "She worked in the cafeteria at the school."

"The kid, Marie and Massey's son." Julian sat back down, planted his elbows on his knees. "He'd be in high school now."

Ryan pulled another chair from the table, turned it, and straddled the seat. "Yeah, but I seriously doubt his mother would see to it he was enrolled if he was here. They would need papers, transcripts under an alias. Seems like a lot of trouble to go to just to be sure he kept up with his education."

"Unless scouting victims that met the criteria made it worth all the trouble," Julian mused. "Marie has a history of check forgery. Maybe she's good enough to pull off transcripts, fake a birth certificate."

"Jesus," Ryan muttered as his head dropped back on his shoulders. "She must have spent every minute of her time in the lockup thinking this through. But, to talk a kid and her aunt into being accomplices to murder? Emily Wilson never had so much as a traffic ticket."

"Maybe they don't know," Julian proposed.

"They're most likely living under aliases," Ryan reminded. "It's not like they don't know it."

"Marie tells them she's in danger. They could be as well if the drug ring she rolled on finds them." Julian slicked a hand through his hair as he looked over at the pictures of the victims pinned to the corkboard. "Now that she's out, they're looking for her. And if they don't do exactly as she tells them, they could all be dead."

"Then what?" Ryan asked, folding his arms along the back of the chair. "She trails the kid to the school that becomes her hunting ground?" He shook his head. "It would be easier to scout downtown looking for victims that met the criteria."

"And spend a whole lot of time following them to find out where they live?" Julian blew out a long breath. "I doubt it."

"Two of the victims don't have ties to the school other than ordering cookie dough," Ryan reminded. "And again, they have that in common with half the county."

"There's a link somewhere," Julian insisted. "Marie Cox didn't get this far being stupid, or wasting her time." He drummed his fingers on the table again, and then he froze.

"What?" Ryan's fingers curled around the back of the chair

tightly. "Julian?"

"Rowan said Shannon Peterson was in the shop a few weeks before she was murdered." He smoothed a hand over his chin. "Check out the other victims. Find out if any of them received flowers, or were in the shop within the last few months."

Ryan's eyes met his twin's again. "The boy, the one who brought the soup by today. He's what? Sixteen, seventeen years-old?"

Julian nodded. "Have your folks check him out." He stood, setting the chair back under the table.

"Where are you going?" Ryan stacked files back into neat piles.

Julian grinned. "I've got a date. I wouldn't bother waiting up if I were you."

Ryan rolled his eyes as his brother disappeared into the hallway. "I'm working round the clock, and he has a date," he grumbled. "Typical fed procedure. Sail in, bark orders, then leave the real work to the average lawman." He stood, dropping his hands into his pockets as he rocked back on his heels. "On the upside, more pie for me."

•

She stared at the stranger in the mirror.

It was surprising how little effort had to be put into a complete transformation. Her hazel eyes were now a startling blue thanks to contacts, her mousy, shoulder length locks a platinum blonde bob favored by soccer moms and celebs alike. Decent food, after choking down prison gruel, added close to twenty pounds to her former painfully thin body. Her face now had a soft fullness that erased years of drug abuse and the agony of mourning the only love she had ever known.

He came to her sometimes, in the quiet darkness of another lonely night, or sometimes in the hesitant, crooked smile of their son. Each time she saw him, she became more resolved, determined those who sentenced him to death would know the same sort of torture she had to live with. She was so close, all she planned falling into place just as she imagined it. Just a few more steps and she would know they were suffering as she had. Her fate afterward didn't matter.

Back to prison? She laughed at the stranger in the mirror. No problem there. What good was freedom now? Death sentence? She doubted it. Jurors were loath to sentence women to even the more humane end of lethal injection. Besides, they would determine she was crazy. Maybe she was insane. Grief did hideous things to the mind, heart and soul. If she was to be proof of that, so be it. As sanctimonious as the feds were, her fate would be one more black mark on their souls. It was another reason to carry out her plans. She would see to it they never lived another day without regret and grief over selfishly using others, then tossing them away like trash.

She smiled at the stranger in the mirror again.

Chapter Seven

It was like stepping back in time, Rowan thought, as she sat at her dressing table.

Daisy lounged in the deep window seat, flipping through fashion magazines as she bit into yet another piece of pie. Her sister was apparently making up for months of eating out of cans and pouches. Fearful Ryan would beat her to it, she hid the rest of the cornbread in the armoire in her room, and was gobbling the pie as if it was about to be taken away from her.

Ava was sprawled on her belly across the bed, making notes on a pad as she checked her voicemail. Back in the day, it would have been one of the boyfriends she collected on the phone, and a calendar crammed full of dates and dances she scribbled in. Rowan always marveled at how her friend was able to juggle boys as efficiently as she did honors classes, basketball, and being head cheerleader urging on the football team.

If Ava didn't do it well, Ava didn't do it at all.

Rowan wouldn't be able to count all the evenings the three of them spent huddled together in this room, preparing for dates and gossiping about everything from family squabbles to friends' wardrobes. They were bound at birth by the friendships their parents shared, connections that continued on through another generation. She wondered if someday their children would know the same blessings, and sometimes frustrations, of lives lived with those who knew them better than they knew themselves.

Ava turned off her phone, tossing it aside as she rolled over onto her back to stare up at the ceiling. "An APB has been issued for Marie Cox, her Aunt Emily, and the kid, Mark Massey. We should be getting as current a photo of each as possible within the next hour." Her gaze shifted to Rowan as she stepped into a black dress that smoothed every inch of her body like a lover's hand. Rolling off the bed, onto her feet, she helped her friend with the zipper. "The boy who brought the soup by today ..." Her eyes met Rowan's in the mirror as she fumbled in a jewelry box for a pair of silver hoop earrings. "Alex?"

"What about him?" Rowan secured the earrings. "Oh, Ava," she sighed, turning to face her friend. "He is one of the sweetest kids I have ever known."

"Still," Ava sighed, falling back down onto the side of the bed. "Didn't you say he and his grandmother moved here a few months ago?"

"Yes," Rowan confirmed. "And I can think of half a dozen other folks who did as well. You know what it's like in a small tourist town. People come and go, sometimes from season to season. There are the rental cabins down by the lake, shotgun houses for lease that turn over as often as every few months." She shook her head. "He's a good kid, Ava. He's shy, quiet ... As far as I know he has one buddy he pals around with. He spends the rest of his time working for us and helping his grandmother out."

"What about the buddy?" Daisy asked, closing a magazine, and tossing it back onto the bedside table.

Rowan shrugged her shoulders as she slipped several silver bangles onto a wrist. "Randy, I think is his name. I've just seen him a couple of times when he met Alex after work. They're into some of the same video games, skateboarding, that sort of thing. I got the feeling teenage boy awkwardness was the basis of their friendship."

"So both are pretty much loners," Ava mused. "Those kinds of kids do normally seek each other out."

Rowan fluffed her curls, and reached for a tube of lipstick. "I'm telling you, Alex is not the son of a serial killer." She slicked color over her lips. She turned from the mirror again, spinning in a slow circle. "Well?"

"Gorgeous," Ava said with a smile.

"Stunning," Daisy added. "Where is tall, dark, and brooding taking you?"

"I don't know." Rowan slipped a compact and the lipstick into a small evening bag. "But it better not be the roadhouse."

"What's wrong with the roadhouse?" Ava chuckled.

"It's where you go to get a date," Daisy pointed out. "Not where you go on one." She ran her fingers through her short pixie. "Surely Julian has matured enough to know that."

"Men don't mature," Ava scoffed. "They're like puppies. You have to train them with treats and whacks with rolled up newspapers." She smiled again. "It's one of the more interesting challenges of being a woman."

Rowan shook her head as she opened the door. "Pearls of wisdom," she sighed. "Y'all have a wonderful evening." She winked at them as she stepped out into the hallway.

"You too," they chorused as she pulled the door closed behind her.

Logan came up the stairs, glancing over her shoulder. "Something I can do for you, counselor?" she quizzed, lifting a brow.

"I was just wondering where everybody is," he replied casually. "Everybody?" She couldn't help ribbing him a little. She hadn't missed the way he'd been shadowing her little sister. As Daisy developed a crush on him when she still wore pigtails, Rowan figured turnabout was fair play.

Logan tucked his thumbs into the pockets of his jeans. "Yeah, everybody." His gaze swept over her. "Where are you going looking like every man's fantasy?"

"I have a date," she said lowly as she shifted on her feet.

"Really," he chuckled. "I won't bother asking with whom." He pecked a kiss on her cheek. "Though I will say my big brother has always been far luckier than he deserves."

"It's just supper, Logan," she insisted. "You and I both know once Marie Cox is back behind bars where she belongs, Julian will hit the road again."

He cocked his head to one side, viewing her through narrowed eyes. "You know sometimes the thought of losing someone is enough to make a man examine his priorities a little closer. At the same time, he might need to know second chances haven't been taken off the table."

"I'm going to supper with him. Past that, we'll just have to see how things go." She fussed with the strap of her evening bag. "I've got my own priorities to worry about, Logan. Sometimes caring about somebody is accepting what they really need. That's something neither Julian nor I have ever been good at. However, I understand more now than I have in the past."

Logan tugged on a long ringlet floating around her face. "I think he does too. I hope that makes things easier for both of you, no matter how it turns out." His eyes strayed over her shoulder once more.

"She and Ava are in my room," she informed, cocking her head in that direction. "Your best bet at luring her out of there is the last apple pie I stashed in the pantry. Third shelf, behind the cornmeal," she called after him as he jogged down the stairs.

Julian stepped out of the guest room, leaning over the railing to watch his brother jump the last three steps as he knotted his tie. He turned to Rowan, his eyes shifting over her as a slow grin spread across his face. "Wow!"

"Why thank you, kind sir," she chuckled as a thrill danced along her spine. "You don't look so bad yourself." She reached up to straighten his tie as he smoothed it over his chest. "I'm hoping this tie means no beer and barbecue."

He gave her a horrified expression. "Wrong twin," he muttered, pulling on a blazer. Taking her hand, he led her to the stairs. "We need to go. We have a reservation at the Lakeside Inn." He smiled at her as they went down the stairs.

"I'm impressed." She shrugged into the coat he pulled from the rack by the front door. He lifted her long curls from beneath the coat, brushing a kiss on the nape of her neck. The thrill spun into a flare of heat winding through her entire body.

Julian twined his fingers with hers again as he opened the door. His eyes anxiously scanned the porch and yard as they went out, the reality of the situation slapping her in the face once more. He noted her expression as he opened the door of Logan's Mercedes for her. He lifted a palm to cup her cheek. "We just met, remember? No past, no future … no insane murderer. We're just a man and a woman sharing an evening." She nodded, and slipped into the plush interior.

Watching him round the car, Rowan wondered if the things he mentioned could be forgotten in the span of one evening shared by a man and a woman with such complications between them.

•

They crowded around Ava's laptop as she opened the file. The same mug shot they already had of Marie popped up. Logan and Ryan leaned in over her shoulder, Daisy licking pie crumbs from her fingertips as she moved closer. Ava scrolled down to a DMV photo of Emily Wilson.

"She looks like somebody's sainted grandmother," Ryan muttered as he scanned the picture.

"It's been my experience those are often the ones you have to watch," Ava replied. "Not much to distinguish her from most other women her age, so chances are good blending into a crowd wouldn't be difficult." She looked up at Ryan and Logan. "Neither of you recognize her?" They both shook their heads.

"If she is in Crystal Lake, she's most likely kept a low profile, and possibly altered her appearance." Daisy took a sip of chamomile tea as Ava scrolled down further.

The grinning face of an adolescent boy filled the screen. The shot was apparently taken from a yearbook, and was dated more than a year ago. He had big dark eyes that brought to mind puppies, and a crooked grin surely destined to break many hearts. Ava let out a sigh of relief. "Well, the good news is Rowan's delivery boy is not the son of a mad murderer."

"Thank God," Daisy breathed. "She is crazy about that kid. Fortunately her instincts didn't lead her astray."

"I've seen that kid," Ryan informed, leaning even closer to the screen. "The hair is different, but I've seen those eyes." He paced across the dining room. "I'm not sure where." He stopped, his eyes meeting his brother's. "Rowan's instincts might not have led her astray, but I'm pretty sure the delivery boy's have. I couldn't swear to it, but I think I've seen that kid with Alex downtown. Some of the kids skateboard in the parking lot behind the post office until one of my boys gets a complaint, and has to run them off. I know the delivery kid was one of a pack a few weeks back, and I'm fairly sure that kid was another."

"We need to call Julian." Logan dug his cell out of a shirt pocket.

"No!" Daisy and Ava chorused as they both shot to their feet.

"No?" Ryan's eyes rounded. "We have confirmation Marie Cox's kid, and therefore very likely her as well, are in town, and you say no?"

"I say hell no," Ava stipulated. "There's nothing Julian, or any of us can do about it tonight. We still have nothing more than Marie's parole violations to charge her with, and nothing on the kid, who if we play this right may be able to hand over his crazy mama with proof she has murdered four women."

"Are you out of your mind?" Ryan demanded. "Do you have any idea what Julian will do if he finds out we didn't let him know about this immediately?"

"Julian doesn't scare me," Daisy snorted. "I agree with Ava. Nothing can be done tonight that can't wait until morning, other than my sister and Julian being allowed an evening together without staring at crime scene photos and wondering what that maniac might do next." She gave Ryan a pleading expression. "You cannot be any more fearful for Rowan's safety than I am. Julian would die before he let anything happen to her. That's the very reason I want to give them some time, Ryan. You know as well as I do they are both at a crossroads right now. All I'm asking is we give them one night without tossing more obstacles in their way."

Ryan looked at his brother. "I guess we could question Alex, and fill Julian in tomorrow morning," Logan proposed.

"I think that would go better if Rowan was present," Ava argued. "The kid trusts her. The two of you would just scare him."

Ryan drew another deep breath. "First thing in the morning," he ordered as his gaze flicked back to Ava.

"Thank you!" Daisy gushed, throwing her arms around his neck.

"I just hope we're not endangering anybody by not moving on this now," Ryan murmured as Daisy planted a kiss on his cheek.

"I don't think so," Ava said softly, turning back to the computer. "I think Marie is through with imitations. I don't know what she's waiting for, but something tells me she's preparing to make a go at her real target."

Logan shoved both hands through his hair as he fell down into a chair. "Let's pray her kid can give us some answers, if we can find him. I can tell you if Julian has to choose between Marie getting to Rowan, or him becoming her next target, it will be no contest."

•

The Lakeside Inn was once the private residence of a tobacco baron, who was also known for running a little moonshine on the side. The fortune he made catering to vices was squandered by his heirs, and when the state auctioned the house off to pay back taxes, a young couple from Chattanooga snapped it up. For more than twenty years, it had been one of the most profitable B&B's in the state.

Rowan looked out over the water as the waiter filled their glasses. Tonight it was champagne and roses. The last time she was here with Julian, it was soda and the orchid corsage she wore to prom. As hard as she tried, it was nearly impossible not to recall their past, or wonder about the future.

It was no coincidence Zane and one of the females on Ryan's force sat across the dining room. Officer Rollins had been happily married to her high school sweetheart for years, and Zane wouldn't consider carrying on with a married woman out of sheer fear of what Flo would do if she ever got wind of it. Rowan wasn't sure who they thought they were fooling. Julian was acting as if he didn't see them, so she supposed she could too.

They ordered their food, and the waiter disappeared after setting a crusty loaf of the bread the Inn was known for between them. Julian all but groaned with delight as she cut a piece, and set it before him. "Mary still makes this every day?" His eyes rolled back in his head as he took a bite of the bread after slathering it with herb butter.

"Like clockwork," Rowan chuckled. "I think she and Brad have turned most of the duties over to staff through the years, but Mary makes bread every morning and Brad won't let anybody else prune the roses."

Julian smiled as he reached for his champagne. "Not much goes on around here without Millie, Flo and Gran having their fingers on the pulse, does it?"

Rowan shook her head. "And what they don't know Zeke or your father catch them up on." His smile faltered, and she reached for his hand. She wondered if it would ever occur to him as much as he feared watching the cancer take a daily toll on his father, being away only made it harder to bear. "No regrets tonight, remember?"

He lifted her hand to place a kiss in her palm. "I remember." He nodded at her glass. "Drink your champagne, and fill me in on all the town gossip you fuss at the others for spreading."

They talked about the highs and lows of small town life, about the joys and woes of people they had known all their lives. They shared sea bass and veal cooked to perfection as she told him about her plans to lease another space next to the shop to expand the lines of gift products and possibly offer event planning.

The Inn hosted at least half a dozen weddings a year, and Kim Lewis' bake shop was earning quite a reputation for cakes that made brides' hearts flutter. As Mary and Kim always steered the floral aspect of any occasion her way, Rowan had already proposed they hire a coordinator to operate out of her new space to make their lives far easier when dealing with jittery brides and overwhelmed charity event sponsors.

"You've never wanted anything else, have you?" Julian asked as they shared a piece of decadent chocolate truffle cake with raspberry sauce.

She set the spoon aside, and sipped her coffee. "There are days it enters my mind," she admitted. "A shipment doesn't arrive on time, the delivery van breaks down, and a cranky customer doesn't understand why we can't add one more dozen roses to the delivery roster an hour after he strolls in off the street to order them." She set the fragile cup into the saucer ringed with hand-painted blooms. "Like it's my fault he forgot his anniversary."

Julian winced. "Poor sap."

"Three years in a row?" Rowan shook her head. "That's simply counting on me to bail him out year after year."

Julian grinned as he planted his elbows on the table, and leaned closer. "You did it again, didn't you?"

She smoothed the fine linen napkin across her lap with a shrug. "Somebody has to save stupid husbands from themselves," she sighed.

"You're a sucker for love, Rowan Covington," he chuckled. Her eyes met his in the shimmering candlelight. "On those days, what else is it you wish for?"

"Most often just time to imagine anything else." His eyes were amber in the golden light, warm, deep amber where she saw as much longing as she felt each time he came to mind. With him this close, longing became an ache fed by every beat of her heart. "But, then I wake up the next day, and realize my life is everything I always wanted it to be." She looked at the roses she knew he asked Brad to harvest from his greenhouse. "At least for the most part," she murmured.

"You know what I wish for?" Her gaze swung back to his. "A deal breaker, something to let me know once and for all the things I have always wanted can come together in a life with no regrets."

"That's not a life—it's a movie of the week. Real life doesn't always come together after an epiphany and all loose ends neatly tied up in a couple of hours. Reality is about choices and responsibilities and very often regrets that are the deal breakers." She felt the temper she considered her biggest weakness flare, and wondered why nobody else in the world could ignite it like he could. "You want a sure thing, which I find a bit bizarre given your history playing the odds."

"You agreed to no past tonight," he reminded tersely.

"It is impossible, Julian," she stated clearly. "You and I can no more not have a past than not take our next breath." She leaned closer this time, watched warm amber flicker into glinting gold. "You're scared, terrified of losing your father, of what a madwoman might do to me, and admitting you don't really have a clue what you want. I can't give you an epiphany and tie up all the loose ends for you. Only you can do that. It has to be your choices, your responsibilities, and yes, your regrets. You hope to find anything real outside of those parameters, and you end up right back on the road trying to outrun them."

They both settled back into their chairs as the waiter appeared. Julian assured him they needed nothing else. How she wished for both of them that was true.

·

The boy shifted his weight, and the skateboard skimmed the curb of the parking lot. He hopped, pressing a heel to the back of the board, and it flew up into his hand. The breeze ruffled what little hair hadn't been shorn from his head, and plastered the T-shirt against his lanky torso as he scanned the parking lot. Why he was making deliveries he wouldn't get paid for, he had no idea. But, he guessed Alex was an okay guy. He was also one of the few friends he made he wasn't discouraged from hanging with.

Alex was polite. Alex helped his grandmother out. Alex had a job.

Yeah, Alex had a job, and he got to go to school. Alex had a normal life without constantly having to look over his shoulder. He closed his eyes, pretending it was the sting of the wind making them water. Things were going to get better. She actually smiled when she told him his buddy dropped by, and asked if he would make the delivery for him. He remembered. He knew what she was like when the drugs were swirling through her system. The pretty blonde woman smiling at him earlier wasn't strung out on meth. Though she was nothing like the mother he remembered, she did resemble the one his aunt spoke of, the bright, smart, happy young woman his mother was before his father came into her life.

He knew his aunt needed to believe it was all his father's doing, that the niece she raised would never have allowed her own child to sleep in a poisonous, filthy pen that could have gone up like a cinder at any moment. He tried to believe all the stories she told him over the years as the memories of his mother made her tales even more difficult to hear. His aunt gave him a home and a chance at a life he wouldn't have had, so he listened, and allowed her to believe what she needed to believe.

Then his mother was back, swearing they were in danger. He asked why now all of a sudden? It had been years since she did the right thing, as his aunt always put it. Yeah, like a reduced sentence hadn't helped her along. His mother never answered his question, just ordered his aunt to pack faster. He was yanked out of the only real home he ever had, without even being able to tell his friends goodbye. His mother kept saying he could home school for now, and maybe enroll in the high school in the spring. He had a feeling she didn't believe that anymore than he did. She didn't plan on staying in Crystal Lake for long. He didn't know why they were here, but he did know his mother wasn't who his aunt wanted to believe she was, if she ever had been.

Opening his eyes, he caught sight of the Mercedes his mother told him to look for as it pulled out of the parking space. "Great," he muttered as he watched the sleek car turn onto the highway. Now Alex was going to be pissed, and it wasn't like he wouldn't miss his one and only friend. Dropping his skateboard back to the asphalt, he looked down at the single bloom in his other hand.

What kind of guy ordered one white tulip for his girl anyway?

Chapter Eight

$\mathcal{R}$owan didn't say a word on the short drive back to her house, and Julian was too preoccupied with his own thoughts to intrude on the awkward silence. Uneasiness he couldn't put his finger on jabbed at his gut, and it wasn't just their sobering dinner conversation. His cell hadn't rung all evening. He knew the recent pictures of Marie Cox's kid and aunt should have been sent by now. Ryan assured he would call. Julian wondered if they had confirmed the delivery boy was Marie's son, and didn't want to rattle Rowan before they had a chance to question the kid.

"So, this Alex kid," he began cautiously. Her head snapped around, her eyes pinning his. He flicked his gaze back to the road. "How much do you really know about him?"

"Enough to know he isn't the son of a crazed murderer," she replied frostily.

He stopped the car in front of the Victorian, relieved to see lights burning in bedrooms upstairs, and the porch light still on. "Rowan, even if the boy is her son, it doesn't mean—"

She shifted in her seat as he turned off the engine. "Alex's parents, both only children, were killed in a car accident when he was seven years old. Two years ago his grandfather passed away. His grandmother grew up less than thirty miles from here. She has a sister in Seymour and a niece in Pigeon Forge. She thought it would be nice for her and her grandson to be closer to family. She and her husband would bring their daughter here when she was a child.

"They rented a fishing cabin most of the time, but they did stay at the Inn for their fortieth wedding anniversary a few years back. Mary remembered them. Alex's grandfather spent the entire weekend flashing pictures of his grandson, and his grandmother asked for her orange and poppy seed muffin recipe. The only reason I was fortunate enough to hire Alex as our delivery boy, before Brad could hire him at the Inn, was because Millie happened to bump into his grandmother when she applied for a part-time position at the library, and mentioned she had a grandson looking for part-time work as well. You and I both know my mother can fill you in on more detail, most likely including a genealogical history dating back to the Civil War."

When she got out of the car, and slammed the door, Julian scrambled after her. "Why are you so angry now?" He rushed up onto the porch after her.

She spun on her heel. "I am angry, Julian, because all of you may have much more experience dealing with murders, but I know this town and most of the people in it. I live here, I work here, I deal with the joys and fears of all of the people you love while you are out there dealing with a life you aren't even sure you want! And I'm angry because it took a crazed murderer slaughtering innocent women to bring you back to me!"

The entire world stilled as her words hung on the air between them. He knew it was the closest she would come to asking, and even now her pride was bruised at admitting that much. He figured this was one of those windows his brother was talking about.

"Julian!" she gasped as he picked her up to hurl her over a shoulder. She pummeled his back with blows as he unlocked the door, and kicked it closed behind them. He was a little surprised, then amused by her collection of curses as he hauled her up the stairs.

"Shame on you, Rowan," he muttered, throwing open her bedroom door. "You kiss your mama with that mouth?" Tossing her onto the bed, he turned to close the door, and flip the lock. When he turned back around, she was climbing from the bed. He decided he'd never seen anything more beautiful.

Dark, gypsy eyes flashed with fury, her sooty curls floating around her face and shoulders as she hiked the dress up around her thighs. Before she could get a foot on the floor, he pinned her back down onto the mattress. He caught her hands before she could claw his eyes out, and wedged a thigh between hers.

"Get off me!" she forced out through clenched teeth.

"What we have here is a window, sweetheart," he sighed as her fingers flexed around his.

"Good." She tried to buck him off her. "First chance I get, I am going to shove you out of it."

"I'll just keep coming back," he whispered against her mouth. "This is where I'm supposed to be, Rowan. I guess I've always known that."

She turned her head, closed her eyes. "You'll change your mind. You'll get antsy, and hit the road again."

He pressed his lips to the length of her throat, felt her fingers tighten around his again. "I don't think so," he murmured into the soft curve where her neck met her shoulder. "I think I did enough running to know some things can't be put behind you."

He lifted his head, waited for her to meet his gaze. When she did, he saw so much doubt he wondered if a lifetime would be enough to convince her.

He damn sure was going to try.

•

Rowan tried to think, but her thoughts became a jumbled mess as Julian tipped his head again to nibble along the underside of her jaw. He didn't mean what he said. Men never meant all the sweet words they used to weaken a woman's resolve. He kissed her temple, her brow, and her eyes when they fluttered closed again.

"I see you like this all the time." He brushed his mouth over hers as she opened her eyes. "Everywhere I go, I take you with me, Rowan."

She made a muffled plea as his tongue swept past her lips, and knew she was lost as he pulled her under the swell of emotions with a long, searching kiss. His hands moved over her so gently, so fluidly until she was completely caught up in his tender exploration. It was as if it was the first time, and she was the only one as he touched and tasted with something akin to wonder.

Like the dreams that haunted her deep in the night, she yielded and gave before he could ask. Their clothes seemed to fall away, her hands gliding over skin stretched over muscle that quivered and warmed beneath her touch. She skimmed her lips over his throat, his shoulder, would have drawn him into her very soul if she knew a way. Framing his face in her hands, she brought his mouth to hers. She gave all she was to that one kiss, and knew if only in that moment, he was undeniably hers.

His palms moved along her arms, his fingers lacing with hers again as he joined them. They stayed there for a breathless moment as the pleasure of being one carried them to a place where only they existed. Then they moved together in a tempo meant to draw out every feeling, every silky glide of sensation. His eyes held hers as they rose and fell away, his mouth catching her every sigh and moan.

It built inside her, shifting, swirling ebbs of desire, until she wrapped around him and held tight as they rode a cresting wave. His eyes were as bold and brilliant as the sun now, his hands knotting in her hair as he moved recklessly through her. She rose up, breathed his name as he surged inside her. And then there was only pleasure as dazzling as the fire in his eyes.

•

Dried leaves crunched under her feet, the wind rustling the tree branches as the moon shot light through them to illuminate her path. She knew the forest now, every slope and spread reaching toward the water. They played here as children, their initials carved into trunks and their memories still lingering in shaded glens. It gave her such a sense of satisfaction, knowing she walked where they found happiness, and the thought of trampling it beneath her boots.

"Soon," she whispered to the quiet night as she watched the last light fade from the silent house. "Soon, baby."

•

Julian shifted, drew Rowan possessively close to his side. The wind howled outside the window, whipping around the house as a storm blew in over the mountains. He listened to her deep even breaths as she slept, his fingers lazily strumming through her curls. It always took him by surprise, no matter how many times the realization floated through his mind. He wondered briefly how often it happened. Was it a regular occurrence for a man to love one woman for the entirety of his life? He didn't suppose so. His father often said there was only his mother for him, and Zeke and Flo, Remy and Millie. He had examples of lightning striking just once all around him.

Still as he pulled the worn quilt up over them, and smiled as she burrowed even closer to his side, he knew to be thankful. Some men looked their whole lives for what he found as a twelve year old boy. He frowned, wondering how many of them would have been stupid enough to turn their back and walk away in search of something more. Maybe his father's example wasn't the only thing he feared not being able to live up to when it was all said and done.

He covered the hand resting on his chest with his, brought it to his lips to press a kiss to her palm. He still had a long row to hoe. Rowan wasn't likely to be swayed easily once she made up her mind. She decided a long time ago he wasn't worth waiting for. However, there was nobody else. He knew it by the way she melted with his every kiss, felt it with every frantic touch as her hands raced over him. He knew passion wasn't enough, but something more than that fed the sort of hunger they shared for each other.

His thoughts were interrupted, his fingers tightening around hers as he lifted his head from the pillow. He turned to the window, watched clouds snuffing out the moon and stars as he listened. There was only the sound of the wailing wind and thunder rumbling in the distance. He rested his head back against the pillow as Rowan stirred, drew a deep breath, and pressed a kiss to his cheek. When she rolled over, he followed, fitting his body to hers as he buried his face in the curve of her neck. She was so soft and warm.

Even the pleasure of having her in his arms didn't soothe his restless thoughts as the hair on the back of his neck stood up.

•

Rowan hugged the pillow closer as birds chirped outside the window and the morning sunlight slanted across the bed. She was still floating along the edge of slumber, when there was a tap at the door. She opened one eye just in time to see Julian striding to it with nothing more than a towel wrapped around his lean hips. She threw back the covers, nearly tumbling at his feet in an effort to cut him off.

"What are you doing?" she hissed, slapping a hand to the door. Julian cocked a brow at the sound of another knock. Shoving him away from the door, she cracked it just enough to see Ryan hovering on the other side. "Good morning." She forced a smile.

"Morning," Ryan greeted awkwardly. "Ah, I was wondering if you've seen Julian. He's not in the guest room."

"He's not?" When Julian snickered, she swatted at his head.

"Well, I'm not sure. But, if I see him, is there a message you'd like me to give him?"

Ryan grinned. "Yeah. Just tell him we're all down in the dining room, and we'd like to speak to you both," he said loudly.

Julian opened his mouth, and she reached over to seal it with a hand. "I'll tell him. If I see him," she added as Ryan turned to go down the hallway.

"You do that," Ryan called over his shoulder.

Rowan closed the door as Julian stepped into a faded pair of Levi's. "Why don't you just holler it from the rooftop?" she demanded, tugging his T-shirt down around her thighs.

He sat on the side of the bed to shove his foot into a sneaker. "Okay," he said as his eyes traveled over her. "I always have loved seeing you in my shirt." He shrugged into another. "I don't know what it is about seeing a woman in his shirt that makes a man—"

"Julian, I would rather the whole family not know our personal business," she insisted, going into the bathroom.

"Right," he snorted as she flung open the shower curtain to turn on the taps. "Best of luck to you on that one, darlin."

She yanked the T-shirt over her head, stepped under the warm spray, and closed the curtain behind her. "I'm serious," she yelled, and then winced as she realized the others might hear her. "I don't want our parents reading anything into this." She heard him come into the bathroom.

"What's that supposed to mean?"

She pulled back the curtain, and poked her head out. "You know exactly what it means." She snapped the curtain closed, and poured shampoo into a hand. "We gave in to a moment of weakness." She lathered her hair. "We're human after all. And we have a past." She stepped under the spray to rinse the shampoo. When she felt a draft, she opened one eye to find him climbing fully clothed into the tub. "What are you doing?"

"A moment of weakness?" he demanded as he ducked her head back under the spray. "Is that what we're going to call it?"

"Julian," she gasped, blinking water from her eyes. "You are going to drown me!" She grabbed a sea sponge, and hurled it at him. "And yes, that is what we'll call it because that is what it was." His eyes flared dangerously as he pinned her to the tile, and the water flowed down around them. "You could try the patience of a saint, Rowan Covington," he growled as he combed wet ringlets from her face with his fingers. "I'm not weak. As a matter of a fact, I think you not being back in that bed under me is a pretty good testament to my willpower."

When her mouth popped open, he covered it with his. It was a searing, possessive kiss that made a mockery of the argument she was desperately trying to make. He released her as quickly as he'd swooped in, and stepped out of the tub.

"The others are waiting. But, we're not finished with this discussion, Rowan. Not by a long shot." He yanked the curtain closed, and stomped out of the bathroom.

•

Her hair was still damp as she strode into the kitchen. Rowan looked around at the others circling the table, her eyes widening when she saw Alex sitting hunched over in a chair. Daisy set a mug of hot chocolate before him, but he didn't show much interest in the thick, sweet brew. When he caught sight of her, he relaxed a bit, but still appeared scared to death.

"What is going on here?" Rowan demanded, pulling a chair up by Alex's. She sat down, and pressed a comforting hand to his shoulder. Her eyes pinned Julian as he turned from the window.

"We just want to ask the boy a few questions," Ryan informed.

"We think he may have some information he doesn't even realize he has," Logan added.

Alex turned his big blue eyes on Rowan. "Am I in trouble, Ms. Covington?"

"No, honey," she assured, patting his shoulder again. Her eyes flicked to Ava. "Is this really necessary?"

"I'm afraid so," Ava sighed. "Alex, we want to ask you about a friend of yours. He's about your age ..." She pulled a photo from a file in front of her.

Alex looked at the picture, his brow creasing with a frown. "That's Randy. His hair is different. It's blonde, not brown, and it's a lot shorter." His gaze met Ava's again. "Is he in some sort of trouble?"

"We need to know everything you know about this boy." Julian pulled a chair from the harvest table, turned it, and straddled the stool. "Start with where you met him."

"We met skateboarding downtown a couple of months ago,"

Alex recalled. "He said he and his aunt moved here from Atlanta." Alex shrugged a shoulder. "I thought it was weird he was from there, and he wasn't a Braves' fan."

"Did he mention his mother?" Daisy asked gently, setting a chocolate chip muffin before the boy.

"No, ma'am. He said his parents died in a fire. I thought both of us losing our folks gave us something in common besides skateboarding. He said his aunt was overprotective, so he was homeschooling for now, but he wants to enroll at the high school in the spring." Alex dusted crumbs from the corner of his lips with the napkin Rowan offered. "I got the feeling he didn't think he would be able to, but I don't really know why."

"Where do he and his aunt live?" Logan tapped a pen to his thigh as he leaned back in his chair.

"I don't know." Alex shrugged again. "We always meet downtown. But, I know they live close to the lake. He's always saying we should go fishing, but I don't have much time with school and work."

"Alex, have you ever taken Randy with you on your delivery runs?" Ava quizzed.

"No, ma'am," he insisted shaking his head. He turned to Rowan. "But, a couple of weeks ago ..." He chewed his lip as he shifted in the chair. "I can't be sure, so I didn't say anything, but I think somebody was following me."

"Was it a woman?" Ryan pulled another photo out, and placed it before the boy. "Could it have been her?" He nodded at the picture of Marie Cox.

Alex studied the photo. "I don't know. I do think it was a woman, but she had on a baseball cap and sunglasses." His eyes flicked up to Ryan. "Her hair was blonde. I could see it sticking out from under the cap."

Logan pulled four other photos from the file. "Alex, do you remember making deliveries to these women?"

The boy looked at the pictures as they were spread before him. "Yeah," he whispered. He laid a fingertip to the picture of Shannon Peterson. "I saw her in the shop one day too. She remembered me." His face flushed. "She said I had the most beautiful blue eyes she had ever seen."

Rowan smiled, her arm circling his shoulders. "I would have to agree with her," she murmured.

The smile faded from the boy's face. "Those are the women who were killed, aren't they, Ms. Covington?" he asked lowly. When none of them replied, he looked at the photos again. "I saw their pictures on the news." His gaze swung back to Rowan. "I remember thinking they all looked a lot like you. I thought it was just a coincidence that I'd made deliveries to all of them." He turned to Julian. "It isn't is it? You think Randy has something to do with this, him and the woman following me." He closed his eyes as he shook his head. "I should have said something when I recognized those women, and about thinking I was being followed." He turned back to Rowan. "I was afraid you would think I was being paranoid."

"Kid, we're not sure of anything yet." Julian reached across the table to ruffle his hair. "But, you've been a big help." He nodded at the hallway. "There's an officer on the front porch. He's going to take you home, and stay with you and your grandmother until we get this all sorted out." He pulled out his wallet, and dug out a card. "You got a cell phone?"

"Yes, sir. My grandmother likes to be able to get in touch with me."

"Good." Julian stuffed the wallet back into the pocket of his jeans. "Give the officer as much information as you can about the vehicle the woman was driving. And if you see, or hear from Randy, or see the woman again, you call me immediately. You got it?"

"Yes, sir," the boy replied as he stood.

Rowan shot to her feet, hugging the boy to her tightly. "You'll be fine." She kissed his cheek.

"It's not me I'm worried about," Alex admitted sheepishly. He glanced at Julian. "You'll watch after Ms. Covington?"

He smiled. "I promise, kid." Alex nodded, and disappeared down the hallway. Julian looked around the table. "I assume you've done some digging at the shop."

Ava nodded, pulling yet another list from a file. "We think Marie may have scouted the victims around town, got their names, and then placed orders for flowers through the shop. All four had bouquets sent to them from secret admirers, each order charged to the same card. Naturally, the card belonged to a stolen identity."

"Is it common for somebody to order flowers and not have an address?" Julian asked Rowan.

She closed her eyes as her stomach rolled. "Happens all the time.

As long as they are already in our computer, we have an address."

"That's how she got into their homes without forced entry," Julian sighed. "She followed the kid to find out where they live, and then showed up posing as another delivery person."

"She pulls a knife to force her way in, or stabs them as they go for a tip," Ryan mused as he raked a hand through his hair.

"The same credit card used to pay for the flowers has been used around town," Ava announced, scanning a list of charges. "Most of the charges are for groceries, gas, that sort of thing." She studied the list. "Here's one for some camping gear."

"She's been staking the house out from the forest." Julian looked out the bay window again. "Probably keeping a close eye on all of us."

Ryan lifted the radio in his hand. "Zane? You there? Over."

"I'm here, Sheriff. Over."

"Get a detail together and comb the woods running along Rowan's property. Do the same across the water at our place. And Jenkins should have a description of a vehicle I want stopped the minute anybody sees it. Got all that? Over."

"Will do, Sheriff," Zane replied. "Over and out."

Julian pushed up onto his feet. "Alex said that kid and his aunt lived close to the water. I'm betting one of the rental cabins would serve their purpose." He glanced at Ava as his brothers stood to flank him. "You stay with Rowan and Daisy. And I mean right with them." She nodded, pulling her firearm from the shoulder holster beneath her jacket to check the chamber. He leaned over to cup Rowan's chin in a hand. "I can't believe I'm saying this, but get your pistol out of the cracker box, sweetheart. And do not hesitate to use it." He pressed a quick kiss to her lips, and then he and his brothers filed down the hallway.

Daisy looked back and forth between Rowan and Ava. "Marie is going to feel them closing in on her," she predicted. "That might cause her to move whatever she has planned along before schedule."

Rowan went to the pantry to retrieve the pistol from the saltine box. She checked the chamber, making sure the safety was on before tucking it into the waistband of her jeans. "Good," she said, looking out the windows at a clear, crisp autumn morning. "She moves too soon, and it's more likely she'll make a mistake."

Ava smiled. "When she does, we'll be there to see she regrets it."

"Oh, boy," Daisy said with a broad grin. "I love tripping up the bad girl!"

Chapter Nine

*J*ulian got out of his twin's jeep, and pulled the denim jacket closer around him as the wind whipped over the water. Tidy cabins lined the banks of the lake, an area for campers and RVs nestled into the thick forest that hugged the roadside all the way back into town. Peak season ran from the end of September through the holidays, so tourists crowded the picturesque landscape millions visited each year. There was nothing more spectacular than autumn in East Tennessee, and new faces was nothing out of the ordinary this time of year.

His brothers climbed out, all of them scanning the area as they made their way to the office at the back of the clearing. George Jones' voice lifted on the air as Julian pulled opened the screen door. Rocking chairs and overstuffed chairs circled an enormous stacked-stone fireplace on one wall, a tall counter stretching the length of another. He tapped a finger to the bell on the counter as he got a whiff of the coffee brewing on a table in a corner.

"Julian! You slippery son of a gun … When did you get back into town?" A giant of a man stepped out of a backroom, his bearded face splitting with a wide grin.

"Hey, Mack." Julian shook his offered hand. "How's life treating you?"

"Can't complain." Mack nodded at his brothers. "Logan, Sheriff. Good to see y'all."

"You too, Mack," Ryan returned. "Looks like business is booming."

"Yep. Always is this time of year," Mack informed. "We've been booked solid since the end of August, and doesn't look like it will slow down until after the first of the year. Maybe longer if we have another mild winter." He lifted a brow. "Now, y'all want to tell me why all three of you found the time to drop by this morning?" He scrubbed a hand over his scraggly beard. "Not that it ain't good to see you, but I got a feeling this is more than a social call."

Julian pulled the photos out of his jacket pocket to spread them across the counter. "Have you seen either of these women, or the boy?"

Mack squinted, and then pulled a pair of reading glasses out of the pocket of his flannel shirt. "Yeah, I have," he replied as he studied the pictures. "All of them, though this one is a blonde now, and not nearly as skinny as she looks here," he reported, pointing at Marie's photo. "The boy too. He and the older woman have been renting 24C for a couple of months now." His gaze met Julian's. "She's a nice old lady. She makes me brownies every week. And he's a good kid. Quiet, on the shy side, and doesn't cause any trouble except riding that damn skateboard all over the place. The other woman visits, brings groceries every week. But, I don't think she stays here with them. I figured she must live around here, and they were just kin staying for the season."

"24C you said?" Ryan glanced out the screen door as his twin tucked the pictures back into his jacket pocket.

"Yeah," Mack confirmed. "What's all this about?" He frowned. "Those folks in some kind of trouble, Sheriff?"

"We're not sure yet," Logan replied as his eyes shifted back and forth between his brothers. "Are the older woman and the boy in their cabin?"

Mack shrugged his massive shoulders. "I haven't seen them this morning, so I couldn't say for sure."

"Thanks." Julian followed his brothers to the door. "And Mack, we'd appreciate it if you didn't say anything about this to anyone."

"Nobody will hear it from me," he assured. "Oh, and y'all tell Aiden and Gran I said hello."

"Will do," Julian promised as they stepped out onto the porch.

"I'm thinking it's going to be way too easy for the kid and his aunt to be sitting around waiting for us to show," Logan muttered as they all looked toward a cabin at the end of the row lining the lake.

"Sometimes fate smiles." Ryan laid a hand to the gun holstered to his hip. "I'll go to the door. Y'all circle around to the back in case

Marie is holed up, and decides to run for it."

"She's not there," Julian predicted as they went along the pebbled path. "She set her aunt and kid up here as a diversion. But maybe they can give us some idea of what she has planned."

"God, I hope so," Logan sighed. "This game of cat and mouse is about to get on my last damn nerve."

•

Rowan chopped onions as she held the piece of bread between her teeth. Scooping the pile into a hand, she tossed them into a pot, and set the bread aside. She thought chili would be a good way to ward off the chill that was supposed to linger throughout the day. Daisy mixed up a bowl of batter for the corn fritters they would later fry to go along with the spicy chili topped with shredded cheese and sour cream. Ava sat at the harvest table, updating her superiors at Quantico about their progress in closing in on a murderer.

Rowan thought how surreal it all seemed. At first glance it appeared to be an ordinary fall day in her kitchen, but knowing what could lie ahead had them all on edge. She tried not to let her worries show. Marie Cox was obviously insane, and if Julian and his brothers cornered her, who knew what she might do. It wasn't like she had the least regard for the life of another, the slaughter of innocent women more than enough proof she was willing to go to any length to settle what she saw as a score.

Rowan's fear for Julian's safety constantly had her mind wandering back to the night before. Whether she was trying to distract herself from the imminent danger, or simply relishing the wonder of being in his arms again she didn't know, and would rather not try to figure out. They were both angry and scared … and needed each other to hold on to. He was right. The feelings they shared were always there, smoldering like a slow-burning fire neither of them had ever been able to snuff out. She didn't regret last night, only wished it wouldn't turn out to be another memory she tried to block from her mind once he lit out for wherever it was he would be headed next.

Ava's head jerked around as they heard the front door open. "I'll get back with you later," she said quickly. Turning off her cell, she dropped it onto the table as she pulled out her revolver. Darting across the kitchen, she pressed her back to the pantry door as

Daisy pulled a handgun from a drawer. Her sister went to the other side of the door as Rowan pulled her gun from the waistband of her jeans.

"It's me," Julian called just before he stepped into the kitchen. When he saw Rowan's gun aimed at the doorway, he grinned. "I have never been more turned on in my life."

Rowan clicked the safety back on, and tucked the gun into her waistband. "Gee, thanks, Wild Bill."

"Oh, Lord," Ava groaned, holstering her gun. "I just threw up in my mouth a little."

"Me too," Daisy admitted, going to tuck her gun back into a drawer.

"Logan and Ryan are right behind me with the kid and the aunt," Julian said lowly. "We thought we would get more out of them here than down at the station." He circled Rowan's shoulders with an arm.

"They were staying in one of Mack's cabins?" she whispered as she heard footsteps falling in the foyer.

Julian nodded. "It didn't appear they were surprised to see us. The boy especially seemed almost relieved. We'll see what they have to say."

Rowan watched Logan and Ryan escort the woman and boy into the kitchen. Emily looked rattled, her face pale as she sat in the chair Ryan pulled from the table for her. When Rowan met the boys' eyes, a shiver ran down her spine. He looked lost, afraid and ready to run if given a chance. Because she didn't for a minute believe either of them had any idea what Marie had done, she went to the table.

"Hello. I'm Rowan," she introduced, shaking their hands. "This is Ava and my sister, Daisy." The boy looked around at them cautiously as the old woman took her hand.

"It's nice to meet you," Emily replied.

"I believe you know Alex," Rowan directed at the boy. "He works for me at my family's flower shop."

"I know him," the kid said quickly.

"He's a nice boy," Emily assured, looking around. "Always so polite." Her smile faltered as Ryan pulled out a chair to sit down. She jumped when he slapped a steno pad down before him, and fished a pen out of the pocket of his shirt.

"Would you like some coffee, or hot chocolate?" Rowan offered, shooting Ryan an annoyed expression.

"No, thank you," Emily replied. "I'd like to know what this is all about." Her eyes darted around at all of them again.

"We have some questions about your niece," Julian began.

Emily stared down at her fingers linked tightly together in her lap. "My niece?"

"Yes," Logan confirmed. "Your niece, Marie Cox."

"I don't know who you are talking about," Emily insisted.

"Just stop," the boy whispered, closing his eyes.

"Mark," his aunt hissed. "I mean, Randy." She glanced around the table. "His name is Randy."

"No, it's not," the boy corrected. "It's Mark. Mark Massey. Marie Cox is my mother." He looked at his aunt. "They already know that, or we wouldn't be here." He turned to Julian. "What did she do? Drugs, prostitution, forgery? Whatever she did, chances are good she's done it before."

"He made her do those things," his aunt snapped. "The boy's father made her do those terrible things. She was a good girl before he came along." She crossed her arms over her chest as she stared at the floor. "All she wants is to start over. But people are looking for her. People he was involved with. People who want to hurt us."

"Mrs. Wilson," Ava said softly, laying a hand over the old woman's. "Your niece is the one hurting people."

"No." Emily shook her head. "Marie wouldn't do that."

The boy frowned. "She let her own kid live in a meth lab," he muttered under his breath.

"Mark!" his aunt gasped.

"It's true," he insisted. "I remember, Aunt Emily. I know what it was like. You don't." He sighed as tears spilled over onto the old woman's cheeks. "I know you did the best you could, and you love her. But, my mother ..." He looked at Julian. "She said a drug ring was after us. She told us they might hurt us trying to get to her because she squealed on them. She said they killed my father, and they would kill all of us too. So, she brought us here, said we could hide out for a while, just until they stopped looking for us." He shoved a hand through his hair. "I didn't believe her, but what was I going to do?"

Rowan took his hand in hers. "It's all right now, Mark." Her eyes met Julian's.

"Kid, we need to find your mother," Ryan said. "If you have any idea where she is, either of you, you need to tell us now."

Mark looked at his aunt. "She wouldn't tell us where she's staying. She said it was safer for us not to know." He took his aunt's hand. "What did she do? We have a right to know."

•

She sat on the cold cement floor in the shadows.

It was sadly familiar, being cold and alone as the quiet enfolded her. She turned her head, looked around the stack of boxes marked Christmas decorations to see sunlight streaming in through the narrow window she climbed through. There was a rocking horse in a corner of the basement. She stared at it. She never had one. It was one of many things she never had. Even more than that were the things she had, and lost.

She would never have a man who looked at her with love in his eyes again. A man to take her to fancy suppers, and spend a night in her arms while the rest of the cold, lonely world faded away outside the window. She was furious when she saw the boy failed to deliver her warning. He tossed it away, the tulip lying by the road like garbage, just as she and her love had been tossed aside.

Maybe it was for the best. Maybe the memory of one last night together was even better. She would remind her of it as she watched the life fade from her eyes with one swift stab. And the best part was knowing Julian Montgomery would wake up every morning for the rest of his life recalling one last night with the love he would never hold again.

•

Rowan fell down onto the side of the bed to bury her face in her hands. She would never forget the expression on the boy's face when he was told his mother was a coldblooded murderer. His aunt wailed like a wounded animal, but he just sat there, staring off into space. The most horrific part was he believed them, knew in his heart his mother was capable of such tragic things. She couldn't imagine what it must be like to know the one who gave him life was able to so viciously take it from others. Her head snapped up as Julian stepped into the bedroom. Hurriedly brushing tears from her cheeks, she stood.

"Ryan is taking the boy and his aunt to a hotel out on the

highway for the night," he said softly as he closed the door behind him. "Officers will keep an eye on them until we have his mother in custody."

She nodded as she wrapped her arms around her waist, and moved to the window. "There was no sign of her in the forest, was there?"

He placed his hands on her shoulders, and then drew her back against him as his arms came around her. "There were a couple of places where it looks like she might have rolled out a sleeping bag." Julian set his chin on top of her head. "We've got uniforms surrounding the house again."

She turned suddenly, her eyes searching his. "What if that scares her off?" she asked shrilly. "Julian, I need this to be over. I can't stand it anymore. She's shattered so many lives, not the least of which her own child's."

He pressed her close again, skimmed his lips over her forehead. "I don't want to scare you anymore than you already are, but she's close, Rowan. I can feel it."

She laid her cheek to his chest, listened to the steady beat of his heart as another shiver trickled along her spine. "I'm not as afraid of her as I am of what she might do to those I love."

He stroked her curls down her back tenderly. "I guess we all have that in common." Cupping her face in his hands, he stared into her eyes. "Nobody is going to hurt anybody you love. And nobody is going to hurt you," he swore. "I'll be here to see that never happens. I'll always be here, Rowan."

"Don't make promises you can't keep, Julian," she whispered as tears gathered in her eyes again.

"I'm not this time." He placed a kiss on her forehead. "I know you have no reason to believe me, but I'll prove it to you."

She wanted to believe him. The hope she would never have to watch him walk away from her again was as much a part of her heart as he had always been. Wrapping her arms around him, she buried her face in his shoulder. For now she would believe. If he proved them both wrong, she would at least have more sweet memories to remind her she just wasn't enough for Julian Montgomery.

•

Gran tucked the covers in around him as he watched the room blur with the haze the morphine brought about. "Maybe I should call the boys," she said worriedly.

"No," Aiden replied clearly, though his tongue felt like it was swollen twice its normal size. He looked over her shoulder to see Zeke, Flo and Millie standing at the foot of the bed. "I'm having a bad day. It's likely I'll have a few more." He took his mother's hand as she sat down on the side of the bed. "Our boys and girls have more than enough to worry them for now."

"They found that crazy woman's son and aunt," Zeke reported. "Zane tells me they think she's likely to make a move soon." He curled an arm around his wife's waist, and then Millie's.

Aiden nodded as he rested his head against the pile of pillows his mother stuffed behind him. "They're all together now," he said drowsily. "Like when they were kids." He struggled to keep his eyes open. "Seems like just yesterday, doesn't it?"

"Yes, it does." Flo smiled, linking her fingers with Millie's. "They'll all watch over Rowan, Aiden. Everything is going to be all right. You rest now."

He nodded again, and let the drug lure him into a quiet, peaceful place where there was only the delighted laughter of children and the loving comfort of friends and family.

•

Julian lifted the coffee mug as he watched her bustle around the kitchen. When in doubt, Rowan cooked. A pan of lasagna large enough to feed an army sat on the island as she shoved two loaves of garlic bread into the oven. Going to a bowl the size of a tire, she tossed a salad, and grated fresh Parmesan over the greens. Just for good measure, she grated more over the bubbling pasta.

Gran called to let them know the old man was having a rough evening, but assured he was resting now, and they were not to worry. Right, he thought, sipping his coffee. If not for worry, his mind would be completely unoccupied at the moment.

Ryan's entire force was combing the county, looking for even the remotest suggestion of where Marie Cox could be biding her time. Julian figured she already got wind of her aunt and kid being stashed away, and hoped it might make her antsy enough to make a move. A move they would anticipate, and thwart before she had a chance to hurt anyone else. He thought about the look on her son's face as he spoke of her, and how little surprise he showed when told she murdered four innocent women. Though Julian was satisfied neither the aunt nor the boy had any idea what Marie was up to, he knew the kid had long ago figured out his mother was capable of horrible things.

"Oh, shoot," Rowan muttered, closing the pantry door.

"What?" He set his cup aside as she rounded the island.

"I would have sworn I brought another jar of blackberry preserves up here." She pulled a cheesecake out of the fridge, and set it on the counter. "Guess not," she sighed, looking around. "I'll have to run down and get one."

"I'll get it." Julian stood, though she was already shaking her head.

"It will take longer to tell you where it is than get it myself," she insisted with a wave of her hand. "Will you keep an eye on the bread? It should be about ready."

"Sure." She disappeared down the steps leading into the basement as he reached for a pot holder. He heard the creak, looked over his shoulder just in time to see the basement door slap closed. When he heard the deadbolt on the other side trip into place, a cruel, cold punch of fear slammed into his heart.

He knew getting through the basement door short of using an axe was unlikely. As he raced down the hallway past the dining room, the others flooded out behind him. "The basement," Julian panted, throwing open the front door. "She has Rowan in the basement."

Ryan passed him as they sprinted around the house. "I've got the door in back, Logan has the kitchen."

Julian skidded to a stop at the small window as Ava halted beside him. "You'll never fit," she hissed, shoving him aside.

"If it's locked—" he whispered as she tucked her revolver into the waistband of her jeans.

"The latch has been broken for years." As he flipped up the smudged pane she all but dove through it.

Falling to the ground on his belly, he peered around the dark basement. He stopped breathing, when he heard Rowan's voice.

"Marie, we think a guard was paid off. Julian, nor Ava had anything to do with—"

"Do not tell me they had nothing to do with it!" Marie screeched. The blade of the hunting knife she stabbed into the air flashed in the shadows as Rowan lifted her palms and slowly backed away.

"They said we would be protected."

Marie moved closer to her as Ava soundlessly rounded a stack of boxes with her revolver poised. Julian pulled his from the holster at his waist, hoping he'd have a chance to …

"They promised if we helped them, we would be safe!" Marie lunged, and Rowan stumbled back against the cinder block wall. "The only one I ever loved is dead." She raised the knife, her fingers tightening around the hilt. "And now they are going to pay!"

Julian steadied his hand, preparing to take the shot. As the blade sliced the air, descending toward Rowan's chest, the sound of gunfire echoed through the basement. Two quick sparks of light from Ava's revolver, and Marie crumpled to the concrete floor. Ava kicked the knife away, and reached for Rowan as she slid down the wall.

"You're okay," Ava said insistently as Marie groaned. "Call an ambulance, Julian!"

"I'm on it," Logan said. Julian hadn't even noticed his brother hovering behind him.

Ryan darted around the house. "What the hell happened? Where are they?" He dropped to his belly at his brother's side. "Ava!"

"We're fine," she assured. "Rowan is unlocking the door now. We're going to be fine," she called out again as she kept her revolver aimed at Marie as she rolled from side to side.

Chapter Ten

*R*owan sank lower into the mound of bubbles floating in tufts along the hot water. Daisy was insistent a hot bath and a glass of wine would ease the chills still running over her flesh. She couldn't stop trembling. Even after she finally managed to get the door unlocked, and Julian swept her up into his arms, she couldn't stop shaking. If he hadn't known, if it had taken him even a few more minutes to realize she was taking too long to get a jar of preserves.

She closed her eyes as she squeezed the sea sponge out to let the water trickle over her head and along her face. He kept saying he had her. It was all right now because he had her. She wasn't sure if he was trying to console her, or himself, but she was sure neither of them had ever been more afraid in their lives. Neither of them had ever been more thankful he had her. Wiping droplets from her face with the sponge, she supposed he always had her.

They were kids playing tag, and fishing with their fathers, then teenagers in the awkward embraces of young love. Before either of them knew what happened, they were a man and a woman building lives without each other. Even then, he had her. Part of her always knew there would be no other. She recalled the way her mother looked at her father, the way Flo looked at Zeke, the way Millie always said Julian's mother looked at Aiden. All around her were women and the men who had them. Forever. No matter where he went, or what she did, Julian Montgomery would always have her—heart and soul.

•

"Julian, I mean it!" Daisy wagged a finger in his face. Leaning back against the bathroom door, she heaved out a sigh at his forlorn expression. "She needs a little while to let it all sink in, so she can let it go. You're used to closing the case, and moving on. She isn't. Just let her catch her breath."

He nodded his head, knowing she was right, but still needing to reassure himself the worst thing that could happen hadn't. He would never forget the blade glinting as it was driven closer to her heart … his heart. "You're right," he murmured as Daisy laid a hand to his shoulder to guide him down the hallway.

"Of course I am," she sighed as they went down the stairs. "Logan says Marie will recover."

"Yeah." They entered the kitchen. "A shoulder wound, and another graze to her left thigh. It was enough to take her down, but not life-threatening. Ava always has been a good shot." He slid onto a stool at the island as she opened the freezer door.

Daisy shrugged a shoulder as she set a bottle of vodka on the island. "It's not every day a woman celebrates a maniac not murdering her big sister." Reaching into a cabinet, she pulled out two glasses. Splashing liquor into them, she slid one across the island toward him. She lifted her glass as he did with a slight nod, and knocked back the shot in one gulp. Setting the glass down, she squeezed her eyes shut as she shook her head. When she opened her eyes, they were brimming with tears. "My God, Julian," she croaked.

He was around the island to catch her as she swayed on her feet. "It's over, honey," he whispered as he hugged her closer. "She is fine. Aren't you the one who keeps telling me that?" He pressed a kiss to the top of her head.

"What the hell have you done to her?" Logan came through the back door to stride across the kitchen.

"I didn't do anything," Julian declared indignantly.

Logan placed a finger under Daisy's chin to lift her face. "You're crying!" He yanked her from his brother's arms, cradling her to his side. "You made her cry?"

"I did not!" Julian defended.

"In case you haven't noticed it has been a difficult day," Logan pointed out, guiding Daisy to a stool. When she slid onto it, he shot his brother a fierce glance.

"You are going to tell me it has been a difficult day?" Julian's eyebrows shot up into his hairline.

"She is crying," Logan fired back, smoothing a hand over Daisy's back as she wiped her eyes with a dishcloth.

"Why is she crying?" Ryan trailed Ava in through the back door, shoving her down into a chair at the harvest table. Stalking over to Daisy, he frowned. "Who made you cry, honey?"

"Julian did," Logan announced.

"I did not!" Julian exclaimed.

"Yeah, hey!" Ava lifted a hand to wiggle her fingers in the air. "Somebody want to pass me the vodka?"

Ryan grabbed the bottle, handed it to her, and blew out a long breath. "There. Now, for God's sake, do not cry!"

Ava tipped the bottle to her mouth before anyone could suggest a glass. Taking a swig, she set it on the table. "Listen to me, Sheriff Pissing Contest," she gritted out. "I have had just about all I can take for one day. And will you please stop shadowing me? I am more than capable—"

"You went into a dark basement, without backup I might add, to confront a known serial killer!" Ryan's face turned a dusky shade of purple. "Of all the dangerous, irresponsible—"

"She saved my life." They all turned to find Rowan hovering in the doorway. Tying the belt of the robe snuggly around her waist, she approached the table. "After spending our entire lives covering your wild butt with our parents, I figure we can now call it even."

Ava closed her eyes as Rowan laid a hand to her cheek. "Oh, Jesus," she sniffed. "Now I am going to cry."

They all jumped at the sound of the phone ringing. Logan grabbed it. "Yeah, we're all here." The shadow crossing his face gave the others a good idea the call was not good news. "We're on our way."

•

Julian stood in the hallway, his head bowed, and the top of it pressed to the wall. He was sure his head would explode any minute, so he figured the pressure would do some good. The others filed in and out of his father's bedroom. When his brothers appeared, ashen-faced and tears burning their eyes, he swallowed hard, and continued staring down at his grungy sneakers.

"He's asking for you, Julian," Logan finally choked out as he dragged a hand over his face.

"I can't," he whispered, rolling his head around against the wall.

"What do you mean you can't?" Ryan croaked. When his twin didn't respond, he wadded the back of his T-shirt in a hand, and dragged him from to the wall to face him. "You listen to me, Julian. This is no more difficult for you than any of us, so you suck it up, go in there, and give our father a chance to say whatever it is he needs to say! After that feel free to go back to whatever life you think you had, but for now, you will stand with your family!" He shoved his brother into the doorway.

It was quiet ... so completely quiet except for the labored breaths of the man lying in the big four-poster bed. There was a time it seemed he filled that bed, broad shoulders that gladly carried the weight of those he loved, tough muscle and strong heart he pitted against the world in an effort to make it a better place than he found it. When Julian stopped at the side of the bed, his eyes opened. There was the glaze of the drugs sliding through his veins, but there was also the utter devotion his son saw each time he turned those golden eyes on him.

"Sit down, boy, before you fall down," Aiden murmured. When his son collapsed onto the side of the bed, he lifted a trembling hand. Julian took it, his heart drumming faster. "It goes too fast, son," he said lowly around ragged breaths. "One day you are a young man with your whole life ahead of you, and the next you're looking back wondering what more you could have done."

"From where I stand you pretty much did it all," Julian replied, his fingers tightening around his father's.

Aiden smiled weakly. "I reckon I did hit the high spots. It's what the love of a good woman will do for you." His smile became wistful as he turned his head to stare up at the ceiling. "We'd known each other our whole lives, but I'll never forget the day I suddenly realized she was different." He chuckled, and then gasped with a sudden fit of wracking coughs. Julian panicked, laying his other hand to his father's chest. "It's all right," Aiden assured, patting the palm pressed to his heart. "We were fifteen. I was walking down the hall at the high school, and I saw Buddy Nelson standing at her locker, giving her that dopey smile of his," he continued. "That may have been the maddest I ever was in my life."

Julian chuckled, relaxing a bit as his father's laughter melded with the sound of his own. "He was asking her to the Homecoming dance." He'd heard the tale a million times over the years, but it seemed his father never tired of telling it. "She said no. She said she was waiting for a fool to muster the courage to ask her."

"Yes, she did," Aiden whispered. "I lost count of the number of times she waited for that fool to muster his courage over the years. But, when I did, it was always because of her. It was always for her." Turning his head, his eyes locked with his son's again. "Many believe the strength of a man is measured in his ability to stand alone. I don't much believe that, Julian. I know from experience allowing another to hold your heart, and leaning on all those who love you is what really takes strength. When you do that, they may think you are larger than life, but really...they are the ones who made you seem that way. You know you're still just a man. But, they sure as hell make you determined to try to be a better one."

"You couldn't be a better one." Julian closed his eyes as the tears stung, and all the air seemed to go out of the room.

"This is your chance, Julian," Aiden insisted, reaching up to lay a hand to his son's cheek. "You've worried for so long about who and where you are supposed to be, you haven't noticed who you've become along the way. Don't shortchange yourself, boy. And don't talk yourself out of becoming an even better man than you ever dreamed you could be."

•

The sun was brilliant on that clear, crisp Sunday morning. It seemed all of Crystal Lake turned out to honor the man who had given so much of his life to their community. Flowers, words of tribute, Amazing Grace, and Aiden Montgomery was laid to rest beside the one who made him a better man than he ever hoped to be.

In the rambling farmhouse at the water's edge, it was standing room only. Rowan waded through the crowd, toward the kitchen with a pie and casserole to add to the buffet twice the number in attendance still wouldn't be able to make a dent in. Setting them on the counter, she turned to find Ryan seated at the table. Ava placed a plate piled with food before him, sat down beside him, and ordered him to eat. He didn't argue, apparently much to her surprise. As he lifted a bite of broccoli casserole to his lips, she pressed a hand to his shoulder, smiled, and then raised a fork to gather a bite from her own plate as they quietly spoke to each other.

A soft smile lifted the corners of Rowan's lips as she turned back to the sink, and glanced out the window onto the wide porch that wrapped the entire house. Logan sat on the porch swing, her little sister at his side as he swayed them back and forth with one foot. They said nothing, just stared out at the sunlight glinting on the water. Logan drew a breath, a long, deep breath. Daisy reached over, and laced her fingers with his. His fingers curled tightly around hers as he slowly let the breath out, and continued swaying them back and forth.

Lifting her gaze, Rowan leaned closer to the window, and squinted against the glittering sunshine. He sat on the newly repaired back porch step, his elbows planted on his knees. He seemed to be staring straight ahead, studying the view she had of the only other place in the world that ever felt like home to her. She was racing down the back porch steps before she even realized what she was doing. Prince galloped beside her, the tennis ball clenched between the dog's teeth.

She stopped on the dock jutting out into the water. Looking across the lake, she saw Julian get to his feet. Stepping into the small fishing boat, she threw the tethers onto the dock. When Prince whined, scampering round in a circle, she rolled her eyes. "Well, come on, you silly old dog!" The animal sailed through the air, landing beside her as she started the outboard engine of the boat. As it spun in the water, she saw Ryan, Ava, Logan and Daisy standing on the lawn sloping toward the water. Shrugging both shoulders, she steered the boat away from the shoreline, and threw the throttle forward.

In a matter of minutes she was across the lake, and Julian was reaching for the side of the boat as she edged it closer. Prince scrambled onto the dock, dropping the ball at his feet. Julian grabbed and hurled it along the bank. The dog took off in pursuit as Rowan killed the engine, and took the hand Julian offered. Stepping up onto the dock, she shook the ebony curls the wind whipped around her head from her eyes.

"I didn't swim," she said, glancing at the water lapping against the posts of the dock. "But I got here as quick as I could." Turning her gaze back to his, she squeezed the hand still holding hers. "I thought it was probably time to come home. It's what Aiden would have wanted. And it's everything I've ever wanted."

•

They watched Julian and Rowan climb the gentle roll of the yard toward the old Victorian arm in arm. "Thank God," Ryan muttered with a slight shake of his head.

"He still might leave," Ava warned. "Call of duty, and all."

"I don't think so," Logan countered as they went up the porch steps. "The last few days have put big brother's priorities in a completely different order."

Daisy sighed, lifting a hand against the sun's glare as her sister and Julian disappeared into the house. "Good. I love happy endings!"

•

Not a single word was spoken as he led her down the hallway, up the stairs, and into the bedroom he climbed a trellis to sneak into as a kid. Julian closed the door behind her as the shadows of dusk shifted around them. She fumbled in a drawer of a bedside table as he shuffled on his feet like the awkward kid he used to be. Lighting the candle, she blew the flame from the match, and turned to face him. She fumbled again, this time with the zipper of the simple black dress. He stopped breathing as it fell from her shoulders, glided down along her body, and crumpled into a pile at her feet.

Beautiful Rowan with dark gypsy eyes and long ebony curls he ached to wrap around his fingers. The colors of sunset played along her olive skin, casting more shadows on all the places he longed to touch and taste. He knew every inch of her, exactly what made her sigh, moan and bid him even closer, even deeper into the sweet madness only she had ever afforded him. He took one step, then another before all but stumbling into her arms. All the pain and misery, the fear and the chill that gripped his heart as he watched his father go into the ground disappeared as they tumbled back onto the bed.

Hold on ...

Two words echoed over and over in his mind as his arms tightened around her, and his lips met hers. Her mouth was so soft, so sweet ... as was the silky skin of her throat, and the velvety flesh of her breasts. She sighed, moaned, and trembled as his hands and mouth played over her. He would drown in her, steep himself in dusky flesh, flashing gypsy eyes, and the satiny heat that drove any hope of thoughts about anything but her from his mind.

They were frantic now, rolling across the sweet smelling sheets as they tore at the clothes between them. Sunset yielded to twilight, the flame from the candle gleaming in her eyes as he hesitated for a thundering heartbeat above her. She rose up to meet him as he sank inside her, their fingers twining and locking as his deep groan drowned out the gasp slipping past her lips. She lifted her head, pressed her mouth to his as her legs wrapped around him to pull him even closer. They moved, heart against heart, eyes fixed on each other as starlight flickered around them. Slow, achingly slow at first, until the need built to an agonizing hunger.

They rolled again, and she rose over him. Candlelight streaked along her body as she reared back, her hair falling in a dark cloud of curls around her shoulders as her eyes held his. Her hips rocked against his, her palm slapping to the pillow above his head as his eyes rolled back.

"Stay with me, Julian," she whispered as every muscle in his body tensed and strained.

"Oh, God, yes," he groaned, tangling a hand in her hair as he surged up into her. His gaze fixed on her face again as he watched the pleasure flicker across it, and felt her body yielding to his. His hands slapped to her hips, his fingers bruising her flesh as he rose up one final time. It was blinding, the flash of heat skittering along his veins as she melted over him.

They stayed there as night fell, in the quiet haven of each other's arms. He cried like a damn baby for the loss of his father, knowing with her holding him tight was the one place he could do so. She reminded he'd done the same for her the day they buried her father. They had been a part of the joy and sadness of each other's lives all their lives. The comfort that brought him on the most difficult day of his life was more assurance than he could have asked for.

So, when they sat at the island in the kitchen, eating apple pie directly from the pan, he looked at her in the glow of the moonlight streaming in the bank of windows in the breakfast nook. Setting down his fork, Julian reached out to brush a hank of curls from her face.

"I'm not leaving, Rowan," he whispered. Her eyes flicked up to meet his as her fork clattered to the pan. "This is my home. You and my family. Our family. This is where I belong." She stared at him for a long moment, and then gathered up the forks and pan to carry them to the sink. He frowned, shifting on his stool as she kept her back to him. "You don't have anything to say to that?"

She turned, tugging his T-shirt lower over her thighs. "It's been quite a week, Julian. For all of us. I don't think this is the time for you to be making promises."

He lifted a brow. "Really?"

"Really." She rounded the island, disappearing out into the hallway.

He sat there, listening to her footsteps falling on the stairs. By the time he entered the bedroom, she was fluffing a pillow. Tossing it under her head, she snuggled deeper into the mattress, and pulled the covers up over her shoulder. He closed the door, and shucked the jeans he hadn't even bothered to fasten earlier. Sliding beneath the covers, he hooked an arm around her waist, and dragged her closer.

"My hardheaded twin tells me the position of police commissioner will become vacant in a couple of months," he murmured against her shoulder. She tilted her head back, her eyes meeting his. "You gotta know how much he wants me to stay by the mere suggestion I be his boss."

"You'd be ready to kill each other the first week," she drawled, brushing a lock of hair from his forehead.

"Probably." He traced the plump curve of her bottom lip with a fingertip. "I also happen to know Ava has been offered a position with the TBI in Knoxville. As it will only be half an hour down the road, wanna bet her being back in Crystal Lake is far more a risk to Ryan's safety?"

Her chuckle was muffled against his lips as he swooped in for a sultry kiss. "I knew she would come back home at some point," Rowan murmured as he lifted his head. Her fingers slid into his hair, her body fitting more closely to his as he rested his cheek against the pillow.

"Then why was it so hard for you to believe I would too?" His hand glided over the slope of her shoulder, along her breast, to the curve of her hip.

"Because I didn't think you would ever believe it." She rolled onto her back to stare up at the shadows the sputtering flame of the candle cast on the ceiling. "Ava just needed time away to prove she was her own person. I guess Daisy does too." She turned her head to watch him in the golden light. "You always knew you were your own person. That's what made it difficult for you to be here. I understand that. It's the same thing that makes Crystal Lake the only place I want to be."

"Well, then," he sighed as he pressed a kiss to her cheek. "I guess I am a testament to the fact things can change. I'm going to tell you again I am not going anywhere, Rowan Covington. Though I realize it may take the rest of our lives to convince a woman as stubborn as you."

"I am not stubborn," she insisted as he rolled her beneath him.

"Oh, baby," he chuckled against her throat as he settled between her thighs. "Look the word up in any dictionary, and know your picture should be right there."

"Don't be smug, Julian," she warned, and then caught his lip between her teeth.

"Ouch!" he growled, jerking his head back. Her satisfied smile was the best reason he could imagine for Crystal Lake, Tennessee to be the only place he wanted to be.

Epilogue

$\mathcal{O}$n a sunny morning in early spring the folks of Crystal Lake turned out again. This time there were flowers, well wishes and Here Comes the Bride.

Millie insisted she was not giving her daughter away—she was seeing the man she'd loved since his first breath finally become her son. Ryan asked what the hell it mattered as they were all constantly bumping into each other anyway. Logan rolled his eyes as Daisy went around announcing she just loved weddings. And Gran, Millie and Flo all cried as the groom clumsily recited vows they helped him write.

He spoke of a boy who swam a lake to get to a girl, and a man who wandered far and wide only to realize the woman that girl had become was all he ever needed. There was a first kiss between man and wife and music and cake and champagne toasts. It was a day of celebration for family and friends that brought to a close a time of grief and mourning. It was perfect, and everything Aiden Montgomery wished for.

Hours later the bride finally sat down at a table draped in white linen as she watched her groom twirl his grandmother under one of the tents lining the water's edge. Kicking off the heels that were killing her feet, she took the glass of champagne Ava offered as her sister pulled up a chair to settle between them.

"Well, you did it," Ava drawled, offering Daisy a glass and lifting her own in salute. "You, my oldest and dearest friend, finally got Julian Montgomery to admit what the rest of us knew the night we watched you two dance at your senior prom. Kudos, Mrs. Montgomery." Their glasses clinked, and they all sipped the bubbly as the band struck up the beginning cords of *Brown-eyed Girl*.

"You wanna dance?" Ryan hovered over them, giving Ava an expectant look.

She turned in her seat as she set her glass on the table. "That's how you ask?" she grumbled, frowning up at him. "You wanna dance?" she mimicked. "That is the best you can do?"

His mouth popped open, and Daisy jumped to her feet. "I wanna dance," she announced as Logan pulled out a chair beside Ava's to fall down into. Taking Ryan's hand, she dragged him toward the tent as he sneered at Ava over his shoulder.

Logan grabbed Daisy's champagne, watching his brother take her into his arms. "She didn't ask me to dance," he mumbled as he raised the glass to his lips.

"Why didn't you ask her?" Ava demanded, watching them spin around in time with the music.

"I don't know, Ava," Logan snapped. "Maybe for the same reason you said, that's the best you can do?"

"Shut up, Logan," she spat. "Just shut up!"

Julian crept up behind his wife, leaning over her to brush a kiss on her cheek. "May I have this dance, Mrs. Montgomery?" he requested.

Rowan stood, taking his offered hand. "You certainly may, Mr. Montgomery." They strolled toward the tent as Ava and Logan both knocked back champagne.

"See," Ava said, setting her empty glass aside. "That is how it is supposed to be done."

Logan glanced at her as he reached for the bottle to fill their glasses. "Hey!" He lifted his glass as his gaze centered on Julian and his wife staring dreamily into each other's eyes. "Do not blame me for my brother being an ill-mannered oaf."

"I don't," she insisted, taking a sip of her champagne. "I blame me for thinking there is a chance he'll ever change."

Logan smiled as he watched his brother pull Rowan closer. "Well, I guess if there was ever an argument for change, there's your proof." He stood, offering his hand. "May I have this dance, Ms. Miller?"

Ava grinned, taking his hand to let him pull her up onto her feet. "I'd be delighted, Mr. Montgomery."

They walked hand in hand to the tent where generations of friends and family celebrated another link in the chain that bound them all to each other.

◆ ◆ ◆

Lisa Phillips

A high school English teacher once returned a paper to Lisa and said he wouldn't be surprised to see her name on the cover of a novel one day. Those words of encouragement rambled around her brain for more than twenty years before she finally decided it was time to pursue her writing passion.

Today, Lisa is a single mother of two sons, making her home in the foothills of the magnificent Smoky Mountains. She is a history buff, particularly pertaining to all things Celtic, and readily admits to an unhealthy obsession with chocolate truffles, SEC college football and the herb garden she's forever plotting.